P9-CCE-359

Francie

Karen English

A Sunburst Book
Farrar Straus Giroux

Distributed in Canada by Douglas & McIntyre Ltd.
Printed in the United States of America
First edition, 1999
Sunburst edition, 2002
10 9 8 7 6 5 4 3 2 1

Library of Congress Cataloging-in-Publication Data
English, Karen.
Francie / Karen English. — 1st ed.
p. cm.
Summary: When the sixteen-year-old boy whom she tutors in reading is accused of attempting to murder a white man, Francie gets herself in serious trouble for her efforts at friendship.
ISBN 0-374-42459-4 (pbk.)
1. Afro-Americans—Juvenile fiction. [1. Afro-Americans—Fiction. 2. Race relations—Fiction. 3. Schools—Fiction. 4. Friendship—Fiction.] I. Title.
PZ7.E7232Fr 1999
[Fic]—dc21

98-53047

For my mother

Contents

TREASURE 3

OUR SIDE OF TOWN, THEIR SIDE OF TOWN 11

SCHOOL 17

MISS LAFAYETTE 41

DILLER'S DRUGS 50

COMMENCEMENT 62

SUNDAY AT THE MONTGOMERYS' 68

JANIE ARRIVES 76

SCOOTER PIE . . . AT LAST! 82

CLARISSA'S ROOM 89

DADDY'S COMING 94

RUN, JESSE, RUN 99

SERVING ON A BUDGET 104

WAITING ON DADDY 113

"I GOTTA HELP HIM" 122

SIGNS IN THE WOODS 127

SHERIFF BARNES 132

THE BASCOMBS 139

JESSE 155

WORD FROM DADDY 174

CRAWDADS 181

MAMA'S GOT PLANS 189

MOVING DAY 194

Francie

Treasure

I did something to that cat, I admit it. But that cat did something to me first.

All year we've been washing clothes every weekend at Miss Beach's Boarding House for Colored—Mama and I. All year that cat's had something against me.

Saturday morning, we went there to wash the linens. I could see Miss Beach sitting on her porch glider as we came up the hill toward her large white three-story house. She had that cat on her lap. Treasure. He'd scratched me four times already.

There he sat with his fat orange caterpillar tail swishing slowly back and forth as if he was fanning flies, his mouth stretching in a wide yawn so that I could see all the way down his pink little throat, past that pink spade tongue and mouth full of tiny razor teeth. Miss Beach nodded at us, then rose and let him spill from her lap.

"Hurry and round up the linens, Francie," she said, squinting at the sky. "I feel a storm coming up."

Mama and I headed out back, Mama to get the tubs ready and me to take the back stairs up to the rooms. I started with Mr. Ivory's room, gathered his sheets, sniffed some of his colognes and hair ointments, and then made my way to my teacher Miss Lafayette's room. I liked her. Sometimes she left books on her bed for me to borrow and then discuss with her later. Sometimes she left a cologne packet from her beauty order. She'd had to go down to Louisiana Friday night for two weeks to take care of some mysterious business, so I knew I wouldn't be seeing her that day—or Monday neither. I frowned, thinking of having Miss Lattimore, the principal, who always substituted for Miss Lafayette.

I studied myself in the bureau mirror. I was waiting to look like I was of some age, but I still seemed nearly as young as my brother, Prez, and he was ten. Prez's real name was Franklin, after our last President. Mama always said I had nice eyes. Now I looked at them closely. She said God had blessed me with my daddy's thick eyebrows and long lashes. I supposed that she was right.

I checked Miss Lafayette's gallery of porcelain-framed photos on the bureau—all of them light-skinned folks like her—and ran her silver-handled brush through my hair.

Then I carefully plucked out my wiry strands from her silky ones.

As I was turning to go, having had my fill of fiddling with other people's belongings, I heard a noise. There was Treasure coming out from under the bed, doing that little wiggle cats do when they're getting ready to pounce. I wondered how he'd gotten to the room without me seeing him.

"Fool," I said, liking the feel of the forbidden word in my mouth. But before I could get it out good, before I could sashay on out of there, that cat ran at me and swiped my leg, drawing a line of blood. It was just through pure reflex that I was able to grab hold of him before he could get away. He twisted and turned in my clutch and tried to reach back and nip at my hand. He pawed at the air with his bared claws, making me even madder.

I marched him into Miss Beach's room at the end of the hall, shoved him into the bottom of the wardrobe, and slammed the door shut. I stood there a moment, breathing hard but feeling triumphant. I wanted to laugh. I wanted to shout.

Then I pushed my deed to the back of my mind and finished gathering the linens from the other rooms. I made my way down the back stairs and said nothing about my stinging leg, though I wanted to show it to Mama—just for any sympathy I might wring out of her. But I bit my tongue on my pain and just dumped my load near where Miss Beach stood in the middle of the kitchen sorting the piles with the tip of her shoe and telling Mama which laundry needed bleach and bluing, which collars and cuffs needed extra attention, and on and on and on and on, like the drone of a pesky fly. She paused long enough to glance over at me and say, "I hope you weren't up there meddling."

"No, ma'am," I mumbled. She stepped away from the piles of laundry and nodded at me to take over. I squatted down to finish the sorting, kind of puffed-up and satisfied and smiling to myself.

Miss Beach was of a suspicious nature. She didn't even believe we were moving to Chicago in a few months when Daddy sent for us. He'd gone up there a little over a year ago to work on a passenger train as a Pullman porter. It was hard work, he'd told us on a visit, serving white folks, even polishing their shoes and ironing their clothes, but if that's what it took to get his family up to Chicago, it was worth it.

Once I heard Miss Beach warning Mama not to get her hopes up. Maybe we wouldn't be going to Chicago, after all. She'd heard of menfolk all the time promising their families they were going to send for them and never doing it. And Pullman porters had some of the worst reputations. Some even kept two families, one down South and one up North. Her words made me have a bad dream about Daddy getting another family up in Chicago and giving them the life he was supposed to give us.

Miss Beach had told Mama that Beulah Tally never left to go nowhere, and after her husband had promised. "Don't count on going to Chicago, Lil. It might not happen." Mama didn't say a word.

Now, when Miss Beach turned her back to reach for the bowl of sugar on the sideboard to sweeten her tea, I stuck my tongue out at her.

By noon Mama and I had gotten the first load of laundry ready to be wrung out and hung on the lines. The sky was clear and blue. Miss Beach's "feeling" about a storm had only meant to hurry us up. We sat down on Miss Beach's back steps to eat the lunch we'd brought: cold yams and lemonade. Miss Beach crossed in front of us, her hand shielding her eyes against the bright sun, and I knew the consequences of my deed were soon to be met. She went back and forth across the lawn, then disappeared around the corner of the house. I raked my front teeth along the inside of the yam skin to get every last bit.

We worked the rest of the afternoon getting everything washed, rinsed, and wrung out for the line. In the late afternoon Mama sent me home to get dinner ready for Prez. I passed Miss Beach stepping out onto the veranda, fanning a face full of woe. "You seen Treasure?" she called out.

"No'm," I called back. It was true. I hadn't *seen* him—lately.

Mama came home fuming. I was sitting on the porch with a letter from Daddy balanced on my knees, the afternoon's events neatly tucked away in a far-off, hazy place in my mind, when I saw her shadowy form moving down Three Notch Road toward our house almost in a trot.

I stopped petting Juniper, our dog, and he raised his head, his ears perking up as if he sensed danger barreling toward him as well.

"Mama looks mad," Prez said from behind me. I hadn't noticed him come out to the porch. "Why you think, Francie?"

"How'm I to know?" I said, my mouth suddenly dry.

Mama marched up to the porch steps, and stood with her feet splayed in the dirt. Her nostrils flared in the dying light as she said breathlessly, "Go get me a switch."

My eyes welled up. Prez sucked in air loud enough for me to hear. I could picture his eyes wide with fear that he was the one who was going to get it.

"Move it!" she growled.

I moved it to the sweet-gum tree on the side of the house, and barely able to see through my tears, I searched the lower branches for a switch that would please Mama. I didn't dare bring her one that wouldn't.

She was in the house, pouring water in the basin, when I came in with a knotty branch dangling from my hand. It felt like a whip. I set it on the table. Mama splashed some water on her face. "Go on in the other room," she said over her shoulder after patting her face dry with a towel.

My lower lip began to tremble at the calmness she'd taken on. I walked toward the bedroom as if I was walking to my death. I had barely crossed the threshold when I felt the first burning lash cut across the back of my calves. My fresh cat scratch caught fire. I jumped and yelped at the same time.

"Mama . . ." I cried, bending to grab my leg. *Whop!* That next blow caught my hand. The pain shot up my arm to the shoulder.

"Have you lost your ever-lovin' mind?" she said, her voice tight through clenched teeth. *Whop!* "You trying to make me lose one of my jobs?" *Whop! Whop!* "I'll beat you till you can't sit down!" *Wham!* The switch came across my behind to help her make her point.

She hit me until I guess her arms got tired. Then she said, "Francie Weaver, why you want to hide that woman's cat?"

It was hard to speak around my fit of hiccups. "I don't know." It was true. I didn't know why'd I do something that was bound to get me in trouble.

"She might not let you come around no more," Mama said. "You sit on that bed and think about what you did." She went out of the room.

I hobbled over to the bed I shared with Mama, the letter now balled in my hand. I hadn't had a chance to give it to Mama. I slipped it in my dress pocket, bitterly deciding to keep it to myself.

I sat and sat, inhaling the scent of the greens and corn bread I'd cooked for me and Prez. I would have to sit there until Mama felt I'd seen the error of my ways.

At one point, she passed the door and said, "You better pray to God for your soul." I knew she was right. Every once in a while I did some hateful things and I just didn't know why.

Our Side of Town, Their Side of Town

The next morning when I woke up, the unread letter was still in the pocket of my dress I'd draped over the chair. My eyes were swollen from crying all night. Mama had left without me, still angry, I guessed, because she didn't even say goodbye. She left word with Prez that I was to come to Mrs. Montgomery's by noon to help set up for her monthly tea. Aunt Lydia, Mama's sister, usually helped at these teas, but her time was close and she'd been troubled with swollen ankles. I thought about the new baby coming soon and hoped for a girl. I was tired of Prez having our cousin Perry to play with and me having no one. Though I knew it'd be a long time before a baby would be a friend.

I fed the chickens and swept the yard. Prez left to go to

the Early farm to help plant cotton with Perry. I started off toward Mrs. Montgomery's. Up ahead Mr. Grandy, in his battered old pickup truck, was heading in the same direction. I could've run ahead to catch a ride with him, but I decided to take my time.

"Francie . . ."

It was Miss Mabel, Three Notch Road's moocher, up on her porch, beckoning me over to her.

I pretended not to hear and kept on walking.

"Hey," she called.

I gave up and headed over to her sagging porch steps, glancing around her unswept yard at the parched weeds. My feet felt hot in the shoes Mama made me wear when I had to go into town. I longed to take them off.

"You goin' by Green's anytime tomorrow?" Miss Mabel asked quickly, grinning and showing off her missing teeth. Half her hair was braided and half hung loose.

"Maybe." I could feel her thinking how she was going to con me as she sat there with her lap full of snap beans, a pot at her feet, and right next to her, her snuff can. She rearranged the wad of tobacco in her lower lip.

"Can you pick me up some snuff? I'm 'bout to run out." She leaned over and aimed a stream of brown juice at her can.

"Green don't let kids buy snuff."

"He will if'n you tell him it's for me."

I dug the tip of my shoe into the dry dirt. I looked out toward the Grandy pasture, at the black and brown cows in a cluster, some grazing, some stupidly staring off. I'd be so glad to leave this road—and Miss Mabel and her cunning ways. I was sick of cows, sick of Miss Mabel, sick of work, work, work. I counted the days I had left in Noble.

A while ago she'd got me to pick up a pound of coffee and put it on Mama's tab. I nearly got a beating for that one. "You watch," Mama said. "That old woman's gonna have more excuses than the law allows. We ain't never gonna get the money for that coffee."

Three days in a row I'd come by to get the money and she come up with three different excuses.

"You never paid for that coffee I bought for you," I said now.

Miss Mabel let her mouth droop in a brooding way. "Go on, then, if you don't think I'll pay you." She made a shooing motion with the back of her hand. She didn't have to tell me twice. I backed out of the yard and was on my way.

I sang a little tune, then dug in my dress pocket to get Daddy's letter. *Ha, ha, ha,* I thought as I opened it. I might not ever read it to Mama.

It began the usual way—no news after the "I hope this letter finds you well" stuff and the part about sending for us before summer's over. I did like the last paragraph:

When you all get up this way, Francie and Prez, all you going to have to do is go to school. And Francie, I'm going to find you a piano teacher and Prez, I'm going to find you a baseball team to play on. It gets real cold in Chicago. There's plenty of opportunity. This is the place where you just have to work hard and you can do anything!

Love, Your Daddy

Piano lessons. I loved just looking at a piano. The thought of learning to play . . .

I folded the letter and put it back in my pocket and continued on to Mrs. Montgomery's tea in Ambrose Park, the white section of town. When I reached the house, I followed the footpath around to the back porch, pausing to pet Portia, Mrs. Montgomery's cocker spaniel. I could hear Mama's busy sounds in the kitchen through the open window.

I stood there a moment, not wanting to go in. Clarissa, Mrs. Montgomery's niece from Baltimore who'd come to live with her because her parents were going through a divorce, was sitting cross-legged on a blanket under the Chinese elm, her nose stuck in a book. She glanced at me, pushed up her glasses, and then went back to her reading. I didn't like her, because she was all the time sneaking a peek at me. I stepped into the kitchen.

"What took you so long?" Mama said, looking over at me from the sink. Last night's beating came back to me and my mouth drooped. "Come here and let me look at you." She squinted. "You wash your face?"

"Yes'm."

"Mmm." She pulled a handkerchief from her dress pocket. "Here. Wet this on your tongue and go around your mouth. Looks like you left some breakfast on your face."

I sighed and did as I was told.

"Now." She nodded at the sink full of dirty dishes. "Get those washed, dry those punch cups." She indicated a bunch of cups upended on a towel on the counter. "And iron that basket of linens over there."

With dread I followed her pointing finger. There must have been fifty napkins, damp and balled up. I sighed again and went over to the sink. At least the kitchen had indoor plumbing and a double sink. At least there was an ironing board and an electric iron with five heat settings.

I went over to the radio, turned on *Homemaker's Exchange,* and started in on the dishes while I listened to the recipe for coffee sponge jelly. The last time I'd listened, it had been mayonnaise cake, and the time before, green-tomato pie. We didn't eat like white folks, that was for sure.

Mama caught that faraway look in my eye, and said, "Pay attention to your work, Francie." Clarissa came in then, licking the icing off of one of Mama's petit fours. She snuck a look at me and went over to the refrigerator to get herself a tall refill of lemonade. I felt her eyes on the back of my legs and turned to catch her studying them with interest. I went to work on a stain on the stove top with the Dutch Boy. When I finally stopped and checked behind me, she was gone. Mama caught me and pointed at the basket of linens.

As we walked home in the late afternoon, I slipped my hand in my pocket and ran my finger along the folded edge of Daddy's letter. Just a few more months, I thought.

School

I still carried my school shoes, at least to the school yard, before putting them on. Daddy had sent them from Chicago in December and to me they were still new and special and too good to be getting dust or mud on them. I didn't care about the snickers I got from the Butler boys every morning as they joined me and Prez and Perry on the road.

"Why you carryin' your shoes, Francie?" Bertrum Butler asked me.

"Cause I don't want no dust on them."

"Cause they from *Chicago* . . ."

"Maybe."

"You always braggin' about movin' to Chicago. Bet you ain't even goin'."

"Think what you want. It's no matter to me."

We entered the school yard and I went straight over to the pecan tree across from Booker T. Washington, the white clapboard building that was our school. Miss Lattimore came out onto the porch then to ring the bell.

I sat down under the tree and brushed off my feet, slipped on the new shoes, and stood up to admire them.

Oxfords. I loved them. Nobody had shoes like mine. I turned my foot this way and that. When I looked up, there was Augustine Butler staring at me from across the yard. She whispered something to her sister Mae Helen, and they both burst into laughter.

I didn't care nothin' about them—or any of their mean-spirited siblings. The Butlers were a large, angry family who sharecropped out near the county line. The boys and girls both were spiteful and always on the verge of a fight. You had to give them wide berth or wind up at the end of a fist. Their father was a known drunk who'd trade his mule for a bottle. All the kids stuck together like a pack of dogs. Augustine and Mae Helen, especially.

Today they were wearing thin cotton dresses with the waistlines heading up toward their armpits, and scuffed, laceless shoes. I straightened my shoulders and crossed the yard, eased past them where they were trying to crowd the doorway. The Butler brothers were taking seats in the back. I sat down at the desk next to my friend, Serena Gilliam, who smiled at me. She'd been over in Florida helping her sister take care of her new baby for

the last two weeks. Serena was a good friend but I o
got to see her at school, I had so much work to do all the time.

"Hey, Serena."

"Hey, Francie. We got Miss Lattimore today."

"Ugh."

Just at that moment, as if our thoughts had served her up, Miss Lattimore bustled in, carrying a bulging leather case that she grasped under the bottom and by the worn handle at the same time. She ignored us while unloading the bag onto her desk: workbooks, thermos, coffee mug . . .

On the chalkboard, in big expansive strokes like she was painting the side of a barn, she wrote the date. Finally, she whipped out a handkerchief from her pocket and mopped at her face.

"Let me tell you this right off." The sudden sound of her deep, booming voice made everyone jump. Serena's brother Billy, who'd been busy whittling on a piece of pine, looked up and dropped his mouth open. "I won't take no mess from none of y'all. And if you know what's good for you, you won't test me."

I frowned.

"Something wrong with you?"

It took a minute for me to realize she was talking to *me*. "Ma'am?"

"You look like somethin's botherin' you." Augustine and Mae Helen snickered.

ore continued and I let out my breath to see where you all are in your studies. Do s I put on the board." She began to cover it with tic problems. Then she pointed directly at me. "You. Get on up there and do the first problem."

It was long division. A snap. *Daddy Mama Sister Brother*, I thought to myself—Divide, Multiply, Subtract, and Bring down. I finished it in a flash, because I knew my multiplication tables and division tables without hardly thinking about them.

She called Forrest Arrington next. He labored through a subtraction problem, but he got the right answer, and when Miss Lattimore said "Correct!" he beamed.

When she got to Augustine Butler, only the easiest problems were left. Slowly and heavily Augustine made her way up to the chalkboard like she was going before a firing squad. She stood a moment, facing the problem. Then, as if it might bite her, she reached for the chalk. It was three-column addition. I found myself running down the ones column in my head. Easy. With the tip of the chalk, Augustine touched the first digit, then tapped the second, lingering. With her left hand, down by her side almost hidden in the folds of her skirt, she tried counting her way to an answer.

There's nothing more pitiful than a big bully of a person being revealed as lumbering and stupid. The beads of sweat on her neck and her oil-stained collar made her meanness all the more pathetic. I almost felt sorry for her.

"You're too big and too old to be countin' on your fingers, missy," Miss Lattimore barked. "You should know your facts. They should come to you as fast as this!" She snapped her fingers. "Sit down. I have no patience for laziness."

Augustine made her way back down the aisle, her eyes on the floor until she passed my desk. At that point, she glanced at me, a quick flicker filled with awful intent. She hated that I was smarter though a year younger.

As usual, the Butlers had no lunch. The boys and their baby sister, Ernestine, played while the rest of us opened our pails and dug into our corn bread, butter beans, and grits. Augustine and Mae Helen sat off by themselves on the tire swings, twirling themselves this way and that to show they didn't care. No past effort on Miss Lafayette's part had got them to accept a handout. They were poor but proud. Long ago I'd even tried to share my lunch with them—but they wouldn't have it. I'd learned that wasn't the way to go with the Butlers.

Augustine Butler was hissing at me. I was pretending not to hear. Miss Lattimore sat at her desk at the front of the class, correcting papers. Every once in a while, her head snapped up, so she could snag anyone who was crazy enough to cheat on her math test.

"Number *four* . . ." Augustine whispered. I stopped writing for a few seconds, then stubbornly went on with my test, an awful anger growing in me. I was determined not to turn around.

Miss Lattimore stood up. "Do I hear talking?" We all held our breath. She squinted at us suspiciously, then sat down slowly.

I handed in my test first, picked up the class dictionary off the bookshelf, and went back to my desk. The only free-time activity Miss Lattimore allowed was reading the dictionary. As I began to get lost in the words, I felt a hand on my arm. Serena was slipping me a note—not from her, but from Augustine, who sat behind her.

Your gon to get it, I read. I folded the note, slipped it in my pocket, and glanced up at Miss Lattimore. She'd be of no help. I looked back at Augustine. She sat there glaring at me.

"Time's up. Francie, collect the papers in your group. Ernestine, collect the papers in yours."

Augustine held on to her test a second, then gave me a slow nod full of threat. Her paper was smeared with pencil smudges and erasures.

After dismissal, I washed down the blackboard, watered Miss Lafayette's plants—I wanted to keep them healthy and happy while she was away—and clapped the erasers out the window, all the while looking around the school yard for Augustine, but she wasn't among the kids who were playing before heading home.

"Come on, Francie," Prez said from the doorway. "I'm ready to go."

"Then go on," I said.

"Mama wants us to walk together."

That was a stupid rule, always having to walk with Prez. I could tell he was mad because Perry had gone ahead without us. I thought of something. "Come here, Prez." He took his time getting over to me, sensing I needed him. "Go see where Augustine is and come back and tell me."

"She's gone home."

"How do you know?"

"I seen her leave."

"How do you know she ain't somewhere waitin' on me?"

"I don't."

Miss Lattimore looked up from her desk and I lowered my voice.

"You go on," I urged.

"You comin'?"

"Git!"

"Well, where you going, Francie?"

"Never you mind." I knew where I wasn't going—down that road toward home so Augustine could jump out at me from behind a bush.

Prez looked at me a second longer, shrugged, and turned to go.

"Anything else you need done, Miss Lattimore?" I had

swept the floor and dusted the shelves. I had corrected the math tests and straightened the books.

"I think you done all there is to do, Francie."

I left the schoolhouse and stood for a moment looking up the road as if it led directly to hell. I walked in the opposite direction. Toward town.

I kept meaning to turn around and go the other way —where Mama's chores were waiting for me, where there was dinner to cook and the house to clean—but I couldn't. I couldn't. The farther I walked, the more I was resolved not to take any chances.

Town felt strange. Walking along Lessing Street, I just then realized I'd never been there before on a weekday during the school year. Clusters of white schoolchildren took up the walk. I had to step off the curb for children who barely noticed me. I stopped at Diller's Drugs and looked in the window, past the display of electric irons and mixers and toasters, to the pictures of malteds and french fries above the counter.

I wished I had some money. I wished I'd thought to get a nickel out of my savings in the can under my bed. I could go sit in the colored section and have me a Coke. I could sit there all relaxed, forgetting my cares. If I was rich and had money to spare I could get me another *Nancy Drew*, since I'd soon finish the one Miss Lafayette had given me. If only I had me seventy-five cents.

Clarissa Montgomery stood with a bunch of other girls

at the comic-book carousel. Holly Grace, Mrs. Grace's blond, butter-wouldn't-melt-in-her-mouth daughter, said something to Clarissa, then moved over to the cosmetics aisle. She lifted a lipstick out of a socket display, opened it, and ran the tube across the back of her hand. She stared at her hand for a moment, looked around, then recapped the lipstick and slipped it into her pocket.

My mouth dropped open. Did I see what I thought I saw? Holly Grace—that Mama all the time had to be hearing about when she served at Mrs. Grace's biweekly book club? Holly's piano recitals, Holly's citizenship awards and perfect attendance—stealing lipstick?

I left the store and moved on, feeling funny about my aimlessness but also a little excited by my newly discovered information. I wished I could be at that next book-club meeting. I wanted to be like a fly on the wall and watch Holly put on her usual airs. I wanted to hear Mrs. Grace brag on her.

As I walked along, I daydreamed, my thoughts finally returning to Mama. She wouldn't be back from the Montgomerys' until just after dark. If I beat her home, I could say I was sick and couldn't get the dinner and chores done because of that.

Naw, I decided. That wouldn't work. I didn't have a fever and Mama could always tell when I was lying, anyway.

Two little white girls came toward me, holding hands. I stepped sideways to get off the walk. That's when I saw

Mama coming out of Penny's Grocers walking behind Mrs. Montgomery, loaded down with two brown sacks. It was too late for me to get out of sight. Mama looked me dead in the face with no expression at all.

I dragged myself over to her with slumped shoulders.

"Excuse me, Mrs. Montgomery," she said. She looked down at me. "Where's Prez?"

"He's at home."

"Why ain't *you* home?"

Before I could answer, she said, "Come on."

We sat in silence in the back seat of Mrs. Montgomery's big black sedan. When we pulled into the driveway, Mama gathered the packages and got out without a word. I knew to follow her into the house.

"Sit down," Mama said. She began to move briskly around the kitchen, putting away the contents of the sacks. When she was finished, she called to Mrs. Montgomery that she was going, got her hat off the hook by the back door, and put it on.

"Let's go," she said.

It would be a long, quiet walk, because Mama didn't reprimand in public. You acted up in town and she just dug a thumb in your forearm and whispered a promise of a whipping in your ear. Mama could wait hours before she acted, and the whole time you lived with an awful dread.

Prez looked from Mama to me. "Where you been, Francie?" he asked me—to gain Mama's favor, anyone could see.

I ignored the question.

"Francie went to town," Mama said. "Now the chores ain't done and we don't have no supper."

"I was afraid," I said quickly.

"Afraid of what?" Mama looked at me full of suspicion. Neither one of us had sat down.

"Augustine Butler was mad cause I didn't give her an answer on our math test." I pulled the note out my pocket, glad that I had saved it. "She passed me this."

"What's it say?" Mama asked. She didn't read.

" 'You're going to get it.' "

"Come on over here, Prez, and read that note. Tell me if that's what it says."

Prez squinted at the note and nodded his head. "That's what it says, Mama."

"And you didn't write it yourself, Francie?"

"No, ma'am."

"Francie didn't write that note, Mama. 'Going' ain't even spelled right. It's spelled g-o-n."

Mama thought about this. She was quiet. Then: "You're not to go into town no more. You gonna have to figure out how to handle that ol' bully, but I want your behind to come straight home—with Prez—after school. *Straight home.*"

There was nothing to say to that. It gave me no answer to my problem, but I could tell by the tired way Mama took off her town hat and went to the basin to wash up that I wasn't going to be punished.

I woke up the next morning with my head filled with

schemes of how to avoid Augustine. I'd start out early and cut through the woods. If she saw me already at school helping Miss Lattimore, she'd just think the teacher asked me to come early.

Prez was trying to spoil my plan by not hurrying, determined to be hard to wake and slow about eating his oatmeal.

"Come on!" I said, pushing his book bag at him.

"I am," he said, squeezing his foot into his shoe. "I ain't even finished my breakfast good."

"I'll let you have some of my lunch."

"What about Perry?"

"We ain't got time to wait for Perry. He'll have to walk to school by himself. Now, come on!"

The woods actually slowed us. We had to cross the creek by walking the flat stones without slipping in, and that took time and care and Prez's constant bellyaching. "She ain't got it in for me. Why I gotta go through the woods instead of on the road?"

"Shut up." Fear made me irritable.

I thought of ways of doing Augustine in. I thought of beating her over her ugly head with a stick, or ripping her hair out, or pushing her off a cliff. Though we didn't have any cliffs around, I could imagine the satisfaction I'd feel in my hands as I sent her over one.

I peeked out from the deep coziness of the forest edge. The school yard was empty.

"Come on," I said, pulling Prez by the arm. We crossed

the yard quickly to the classroom door. It was locked. I tried it twice, my heart sinking. Prez ran around to the window. He had to jump up to peek in.

"She's in there," he said.

"Who?"

"Miss Lattimore. She's in there at her desk."

"What's she doing?"

He jumped up again. "Nothin'."

"Nothing?"

"Just drinkin' a cup of tea or coffee or somethin'."

I went back to the door and tapped lightly. I waited, listening. When the door opened, I stepped back, speechless. Miss Lattimore, with a steaming cup in her hand, looked annoyed.

"What is it, Francie?"

"I just wanted to know if you needed any help?"

"Can't say I do—right now. You go on and play."

How was I supposed to go and play? I sat down on the steps, feeling miserable. Prez was happy—he had the tire swing all to himself.

Then I noticed someone coming up the road. I could tell by the loping walk it wasn't Augustine. I shaded my eyes against the morning sun and closed my mouth, which had dropped open. It was a boy. A big boy. He walked right into the school yard, stopped for a few seconds to look around, and walked over to me, bold as you please.

His kinky hair was brushed back and packed down like

it had been under a stocking cap all night. His overalls and shirt were tattered but clean. He was darker than me, a reddish kind of dark. He didn't look me in the eye.

"What time this school start?"

"In a little while," I said. He put one foot on the bottom step and looked off like he was trying to cover up some embarrassment. Prez hopped off the swing and came over to stare at him. He was still young enough to get away with it.

"Who are you?" Prez said.

"Jesse Pruitt."

I was secretly happy that Prez was so outright nosy.

"I ain't never seen you before. Where you from?"

"Over in New Carlton." He stopped to give Prez the once-over. Then something seemed to smile in his eyes but not on his lips. "Ain't no school in New Carlton."

"Everybody know that."

"Yea," he said. Then there was silence all around.

As soon as the yard began to fill up, Jesse went over to a tree stump to sit and wait. Finally, Miss Lattimore came out and rang the bell. I dashed inside.

From the safety of my seat, I watched my classmates file in, the strange boy hanging back, I noted, in the doorway. Each person looked up at him as they passed, wondering who he was and why he was there. Augustine finally arrived, and she stared openly at him even after she sat down, seeming to have forgotten all about me.

Miss Lattimore took her seat, shuffled some papers,

then looked over her glasses at the boy. "You here for school?"

He didn't look her in the eye.

"Yes'm."

"What's your name?"

"Jesse Pruitt."

"Pruitt. I ain't heard that name before. Where's your people?"

"We stay up by New Carlton," he mumbled.

"How old are you, Jesse Pruitt?"

He didn't answer right away. She waited, tilting her head to the side, like she was expecting him to lie. He said nothing. Augustine and Mae Helen snickered behind their hands. "Well, Jesse Pruitt, can you hear? I asked you a question."

"Sixteen," he said quietly. So quietly that I didn't know if I heard him right. Yes, there was something older about him and there was something serious, something weighing on him.

"Come again?" Miss Lattimore said. Jesse would be in an age group all by himself.

"I'm sixteen," he repeated, his voice loud now as if he had a point to prove. I felt sorry for him standing there like he had no kin, no friends, not a soul in his corner.

"You're a big boy. Take that seat in the back. I don't want you to be blocking the view from the little ones. Pass out the readers, Francie."

I got up to do as I was told. Augustine took hers out

of my hand with a little snatch. I placed one on Jesse Pruitt's desk and gave him a smile to encourage him. He looked at the book's cover, leaving it as I had put it. Upside down. I knew at that moment he was like Mama. He couldn't read.

Miss Lattimore got the lower grades practicing their printing, the middle grades their cursive, then she had us turn to *Hiawatha* in our books. Reading aloud was the most boring thing I had to endure every morning, because Mae Helen, Augustine, and several others who'd never learned to read too good would take ten years to drag through one sentence. The teacher had to tell them every other word. Then the next morning they would repeat the very same mistakes. Some of them were thick as posts. My turn would be over before I knew it, after waiting all morning for the teacher to get to me.

This time was different, because Miss Lattimore was making her way down the row to Jesse Pruitt. He came after Serena's brother J. Dean, who took minutes and minutes to limp through five lines. Then: "Okay, Jesse Pruitt, let's see what you can do. Take it from there."

I looked back. His book was still closed and upside down. He touched it but did not open it. "I ain't learned to read," he said, loud enough for there to be no doubt about what was said. Everyone whipped around then. Even the poor readers, probably glad that there was finally someone worse off than them.

"You don't read . . ." Miss Lattimore adjusted her

glasses, trying to figure out what to do with this big person who never learned to read. "You can't read at all?"

"I never went to school regular."

"I see. Well, you comin' here after school's been in session for months. I don't have time to coddle you. Francie's a good reader. Maybe she can help you. Maybe she can't." She looked over at me. "Francie?"

"Yes, ma'am, I'll help him." I looked back at Jesse and smiled, but he was sitting there staring at his hands.

"Now, you know your alphabet?"

"My ABCs?"

"Yea—your ABCs." Jesse Pruitt and I had stayed behind after everyone had been sent home. Miss Lattimore was grading quizzes at her desk, not seeming to pay any mind to us.

"My mama taught me."

"You know the sounds of the letters?"

"No—I don't think so."

I looked at him. It was going to be a long, hard row to hoe, I decided.

By the time I'd taken him through the sounds of the consonants so that he could remember them, I'd changed my mind. Jesse Pruitt wasn't no dummy, and I was going to teach him to read. The idea gave me butterflies in my stomach.

I looked out the window. The school yard was nearly empty now, and Miss Lattimore was packing up to go.

Prez was kicking a pebble around. He was soon going to grow tired of waiting on me every day. I wished Perry would stick around with him.

"How come that boy never went to school?" Prez and I were hurrying home to get there in time to do our chores.

"Mama never went," I said.

"How come Mama never went?"

"She had to take care of all her brothers and sisters when her mama died."

For a moment, I felt sad for Mama—her never going to school. But then my sadness vanished as soon as I remembered I was teaching someone to *read.* I quickened my pace, determined to keep Mama satisfied with my work so I could keep staying after school, helping Jesse Pruitt. I was feeling so good, thinking about this, I forgot all about Augustine.

And suddenly there she was. Augustine stepped in front of me with Mae Helen right behind her. She wore her ugly grin on her face, like this was something she'd been planning all day. I was more surprised than scared. Then I felt a prick of anger. Prez looked from me to her.

Without a word, I tried to go around her, but Augustine blocked me, and Mae Helen joined her to widen the barrier.

"You think you so cute, don't you—just cause you think you movin' up to Chicago." Augustine turned her head and spit on the ground. "Shoot, it ain't so special. I got a cousin up there and it ain't so hot."

"Yea," Mae Helen said, inching closer. She was bigger than Augustine, with a halo of unruly hair that stood out all around her face. I weighed her role in this, deciding I couldn't fight one of them—let alone both.

"I never said it was special and I don't think I'm cute," I said, my voice breaking and sounding frightened to my own ears.

"You shoulda give me that answer."

"Miss Lattimore would've torn up my paper," I said.

"So?"

Augustine didn't care about no answer. She just didn't like me. She was simply giving herself something to go on—giving herself a reason to beat me up.

I stepped back, knocking into Prez. Augustine, taller than me, leaned forward, her arms behind her a bit, her chest out. She brought her face close to mine. It was like a dance. She'd said her ugly words, and next she'd be giving me a hard shove. I braced myself for it, so when it came, it took more effort than she expected to knock me down. But Augustine outweighed me by about twenty pounds. I fell hard on my elbows, scraping them on the gravel. Both girls laughed. When I tried to get up, Mae Helen pushed me down.

"Come on—get up. Ain't you gonna get up?" Mae Helen looked at Augustine, I guess for instructions on what to do next.

Prez began to cry, taking Mae Helen's attention off me for a second. I hurried to stand up. "Aw, no you don't," Augustine said, readying herself to shove me again. But just then Jesse, appearing out of nowhere it seemed, grabbed her from behind, nearly lifting her off her feet before setting her aside. She went down on her butt hard, her eyes wide with surprise. She struggled to get up, but Jesse Pruitt held her down by the top of the head, so all she could do was get purplish with the effort to push against his big flat palm. Prez laughed, suddenly feeling brave.

I brushed the back of my dress off.

"Now," Jesse told Mae Helen, "you go on home." He turned to Augustine. "You, too," he said. He didn't even sound angry.

Mae Helen helped her sister to her feet. They started up the road—slowly, shooting mean stares back at me to pretend they weren't scared, anyhow. I met every one of their stares. To show I wasn't scared, neither.

"You okay?" Jesse asked.

"Where'd you come from?"

"I followed you."

"How come?"

"I heard them talking about all they were going to do to you. I thought it was just talk. But I decided to see for myself. So I come this way, stayin' behind you." He looked past me.

"I'm fine," I said.

"I'ma go, then."

I brushed away more dirt and twigs that were clinging to my dress. "Thanks," I said and watched him walk away. Me and Prez started for home.

More important things came into my thoughts, though. I'd have to really hurry now. With all the delays, it was going to be nearly impossible to rush through everything I needed to get done before Mama arrived home hot, tired, and irritated.

I tutored Jesse every day the rest of the week. Miss Lattimore, busy with her teaching and principal duties, bustled in and out of the classroom and hardly seemed to notice us. I liked teaching Jesse for two reasons: I liked watching his progress, and he kept me safe from Augustine.

I surprised myself. I could tutor Jesse for thirty minutes, run home, and get every one of my chores done and the dinner on the stove by the time Mama was walking up the road toward home. Course, that first night Mama had caught sight of my scraped elbows and said, "What happened to you?" I was in a pitiful state, like someone always doing battle and getting a new wound every time she turned around. Cat scratches, welts from a whipping, and now scraped elbows that promised to crack and sting fiercely whenever I bent my arms.

"I hurt myself," I'd said simply and Mama was too tired to question me further.

"What's that?" Jesse asked me the following Monday.

"What?"

"That," he said, laying his finger on the picture of an orange grove. Slowly and painfully, he was making his way through *The Little Red Hen.* I had to bite my tongue to keep from yawning. It took a lot of patience not to correct him, to wait and let him sound the words out himself. Sometimes I had to tell him. Then he'd repeat it four or five times, even closing his eyes while he said it to see it in his mind. But I never had to tell him that word again.

"That's what you call an orange grove. We don't have any here." I looked out the schoolhouse window at the trees we grew here. Pine and pecan, peach and sweet gum. No orange.

"Where they have orange groves?"

"They have them in Florida and California."

"Where's this California?"

"On the other side of the country. Right where the Pacific Ocean is."

"Where's that?"

I looked in his earnest face. He didn't know where the Pacific Ocean was. I got up and checked the hall toward the small room Miss Lattimore used as an office. Then I got the atlas off the front desk and opened it to the map of the United States. Jesse leaned over me. "We're here," I said, showing him where Alabama was. "And the Pacific Ocean is here." I ran my finger slowly across the map to show what a big country it was we lived in. "It's two thousand miles away."

"Two thousand miles," he repeated and pulled at his sleeve. "I'ma go there one day—where they grow oranges on trees." He thought about his own words for a moment.

Then he gave a short nod, like he was settling it in his mind.

He stood and started for the door, just as he did every day, saying that was all the time he could spare.

The next day, Jesse was late for the first time. In the middle of multiplication drills, he entered, head down. Some of the kids stared as he slunk to his seat, waiting to see if he'd get yelled at. But Miss Lattimore didn't miss a beat. She just went on calling on us and snapping her fingers if we hesitated. She didn't call on Jesse and he didn't volunteer. It seemed she was letting him make his way.

The next day, Miss Lattimore had him listen to the second-graders read *Little Red Hen* and follow along as best he could. Later, she gave him a slate to practice writing letters from his penmanship book and only called on him when she couldn't avoid it. Any giggling was met with a piercing stare over her glasses.

Finally on Friday I asked Jesse a question that had been nagging at me. "How do you get all the way here from New Carlton?"

"I walk."

I thought about this. New Carlton was six or seven miles away. He'd have to start out at sunrise to get here on time.

"Why did you want to go to school? Now?"

"I always wanted to go." His eyes left the window and settled on me almost defiantly. "My daddy needed me to work in the fields. I'm the oldest." He shrugged. "My mama always wanted me to go, too."

"You going for your mama."

His mouth quivered and he lowered his eyes. "She died."

"You don't have a mama?"

He seemed to be struggling to compose himself. Finally, he managed to say, "She died last winter—and I always promised her I'd get some schooling. So that's why I come here."

"Who do you live with now?"

"My daddy and my younger brother and younger sister."

"Who takes care y'all?"

"We all take care of ourselves."

That was the loneliest thing I'd ever heard. Even with all the work I had to do, I never thought I was the only one taking care of me.

"I want you to come home with me—for dinner."

He looked surprised. "I can't do that."

"Why?"

"I'm expected at home. I gotta get there before the sun go down. I got a lot of work that has to be done yet." He stood then. "Or my daddy will stop me from comin' for sure."

Miss Lafayette

Mama argued my case and I was allowed to return to Miss Beach's on Saturday.

All the way there, I had to hear Mama's lecture. "I need your help, so stay out of the way of that cat and just do your work."

"Yes, Mama," I said, though I was hardly listening. Miss Lattimore had announced that Miss Lafayette would be back on Monday, so my mind was on seeing her, telling her about Jesse. Maybe she even had a present for me.

"Are you listening to me, Francie?"

"Yes'm."

Miss Beach was up on her porch as usual—Treasure curled on her lap, enjoying Miss Beach's long and slow strokes down his back. When we got within earshot, Mama called out brightly, "Mornin', Miss Beach! Nice day for doin' laundry, ain't it?"

Miss Beach looked up, nodded, then narrowed her eyes at me.

"Francie's got somethin' she wants to tell you," Mama said, nudging me.

"I'm really sorry, Miss Beach, for what I did to that cat." Mama elbowed me in the side. "And I'm never going to put him in your wardrobe again."

Miss Beach, who was busy checking something in Treasure's fur, looked up. "You better not," she said. Then, as if she'd just thought of it, she said, "And don't go pestering Miss Lafayette."

I said nothing, but I felt as if I would burst with joy. Miss Lafayette was really home!

I hurried around the back and started up the stairs. I listened for a few seconds at Miss Lafayette's door, then tapped on it.

"Come in, Francie."

I stepped in, feeling suddenly shy. Miss Lafayette was still in bed. I'd never seen her in a nightgown before. Her pecan-colored hair, always up and out of the way, was hanging down over her shoulder to her waist. She sat propped against pillows in a white gown with tiny roses around the neck and wrists. She looked as fragile as a china teacup. She had a book face-down on her lap.

She smiled at me. I stayed near the door, my hand

still on the knob. "Hello, Miss Lafayette. I'm glad you're back."

"Have you all been showing Miss Lattimore you have some home training from ol' Miss Lafayette?"

"You're not old."

She pulled a flat package out from somewhere under the covers, wrapped in brown paper. "Been waiting for you." I pressed my lips together to hide my pleasure. "Here." She held it out to me.

I walked to her bedside. "You sick?"

She waved the question away. "Sit down," she said, patting the strip of space next to her, and I eased down on the edge, feeling funny about sitting there.

She chuckled. "I'm not going to bite you, Francie. Here," she said again.

Carefully, I took the package out of her hand and unwrapped it, trying not to tear the paper.

It was a book. I knew it would be. Miss Lafayette knew how I loved books. She knew I'd started my own little library with the books she'd given me.

The Dream Keeper by Langston Hughes.

"The poet," I said.

Miss Lafayette looked at me closely and recited:

> *"Hold fast to dreams*
> *For if dreams die*
> *Life is a broken-winged bird*
> *That cannot fly."*

I flipped through the pages. "I'ma read it on my hill."

"While you wait for the train to go by?"

"No, I eat my Scooter Pie while it goes by. Then I read."

She laughed.

"Thank you, Miss Lafayette." I ran my hand over the cover.

"What have you been up to?"

"We got a new boy, Miss Lafayette. His name is Jesse Pruitt and he's sixteen and he can't read."

"Oh?" She cocked her head with interest.

"I'm teaching him."

"Are you doing a good job?"

"I think so."

"Good."

I heard my name being called then. Miss Beach—calling up to see what was taking me so long. Miss Lafayette nodded toward the laundry bag hanging on the bedpost. I looked back at her before going out the door. "Will you be at school on Monday?"

She winked at me.

"Is she gonna be there?" Prez said as we walked with Perry to school Monday morning.

"I said she was."

"You know for sure?" Perry asked.

"Don't no one ask me again."

We turned into the yard just as Miss Lafayette stepped

out to ring the bell. Prez and I grinned at each other at the same time.

How different the two teachers were. In her smooth, gentle manner, Miss Lafayette leaned on the edge of her desk, looked us over, and said, "I've missed you so."

"Why were you gone so long?" Perry burst out, and I could have smacked him for his rudeness.

"It really wasn't that long—only two weeks." Miss Lafayette blushed almost crimson.

"Felt like a long time," Bertrum mumbled.

Miss Lafayette looked at her watch. "Let's get busy. Bertrum, please pass out the readers."

I sighed. Just then Jesse arrived—late as usual, but this time I knew why.

He stopped in the doorway, not knowing what to think about Miss Lafayette's presence. Carefully he made his way to the back of the room.

"Are you Jesse?" Miss Lafayette asked.

He was just sinking into his seat. Now he stood up quickly. "Yes, ma'am."

"Are you always late, or is this an exception?"

"I'm late almost every day, ma'am."

"May I ask why?"

Jesse stood blinking at Miss Lafayette, not knowing how to take such politeness coming from an adult.

"I come from New Carlton and I can't leave as early as I need to, cause I got chores to do."

I'd been looking from one to the other. Now I switched back to Miss Lafayette. She frowned, slightly.

"That's a long way you walk."

"Yes, ma'am."

Noticing he was empty-handed, she asked, "Where's your lunch?"

Jesse didn't answer. He looked out the window, then back at her, then down at the floor.

"Never mind. Please sit down."

I'd tried to share my lunch with Jesse when after a day or so I noticed he had nothing. But he always acted like he wasn't a bit hungry. Then on Friday I'd pretended to be full, with corn bread left over. He took it then, just so it wouldn't "go to waste."

At midday, Miss Lafayette dismissed us for lunch but held Jesse back. I knew she'd try to coax him to take some of her lunch. And I was sure he wouldn't take it. He'd be just like those proud Butlers—pretend he wasn't hungry. I'd ask him to come to our house for dinner again.

Miss Lafayette quietly corrected papers at the front of the class while I tutored Jesse in the back. I bit my lip to stay alert while he struggled through a paragraph, putting his finger on each word as he went along at a pace that was torture. I still loved the notion of teaching someone to read, but it sure did take patience.

"Jesse," I said, when he stopped to take a breath. "Can you come for dinner on Friday?"

He stared at the page he'd been reading.

"Friday. Cause you don't have to go to school on Saturday—maybe you can put some things off?"

I felt a little anger rise up in him and immediately regretted being so pushy.

"Why you always askin' me to do something I can't. It just makes me feel bad." He hadn't looked up yet. He clenched his fists. "I said I can't do it." His voice rose enough for Miss Lafayette to look up and watch us a moment.

"I'm sorry," I told him.

"I can't do it." He got up quickly then. "Time for me to go," he said, pulling himself up out of his chair. He didn't even bother closing the book before he walked out of the room.

Mr. Pruitt came the last Monday in April to take Jesse out of Booker T.

J. Dean had led the Pledge of Allegiance and we'd just sat down to work on our readers when a strange man appeared in the doorway in work overalls, holding his hat. Jesse had arrived on time and sat hunched over his book, seemingly with no thoughts of nothing else. The man wore a hard expression on his face. He looked directly at Jesse. Jesse must have felt eyes on him because he glanced up, and immediately flinched. The man lifted his chin, just a little, but it was enough to have Jesse scrambling out of his chair and making his way up the aisle. He didn't even get to the door good when his daddy—it didn't take long for me to realize he was Jesse's daddy—reached out and grabbed his arm. He gave him a hard shove and Jesse, looking as weak as a sick kitten, let himself be pushed out the door and down the steps. We all watched them through the window hurrying along the road. Miss Lafayette stood and watched with us, saying nothing.

Then she sighed heavily. "Let's get back to work," she said.

"Who was that?" Serena whispered to me.

"His daddy, I'ma bet."

For the rest of the day I hoped to see Jesse walk back through our classroom door, but when 3:00 came and he still hadn't returned, I feared he wasn't ever coming back.

For the rest of the week I watched for him. I'd frequently check the window, picturing him loping up the road like the first time I saw him. Then I'd imagine him coming through the door after we'd all settled with our readers. He didn't come.

His absence wasn't lost on Augustine. Toward the end of the week, she squatted down beside me while I was waiting my turn to play the winner in a game of jacks. "Where's your friend?"

I didn't answer.

"He comin' back?"

"Sure. When he can get away." She considered this, checking me closely to see if I was lying. "It's planting time," I continued. "He's gotta help his daddy right about now. But he's coming back and he's my friend."

She stood up and looked down at me. She snorted. "Betcha he ain't comin' back," she said.

I swallowed and put my eyes on Serena and Viola's game like I didn't care one way or the other. But I did care—a lot.

Diller's Drugs

"Mama," I said on Saturday, as we were hurrying along to Miss Beach's.

"What, baby?" She had that far-off look in her eye. She'd gotten a letter from Daddy and this time she'd fished it out the mailbox first and had me read it to her.

It was full of the usual promises. Promises that he was going to send for us. That he was going to set us up in Chicago with our own house. That Mama wouldn't have to do day work and laundry no more cause he didn't want that for a wife of his, and how Prez and me were just going to have to go to school. No more scrubbing other people's clothes and serving at people's parties for me and no more planting and picking cotton for Prez. And, on top of that, I was going to get those piano lessons I was wanting for a long, long time. I knew the promises by heart because I'd been hearing them since a year ago March, when Daddy left the pulp mill to go up to Chicago, but sometimes I didn't know how much I believed them.

When my chores were done and I could go sit under my pecan tree up from the railroad tracks to read, then I'd think about the promises and life up North.

This time, money had come. Mama had given me and Prez a nickel apiece. I knew what I was going to do with mine. I was going to buy me a Scooter Pie, get my *Nancy Drew* from home, and go read and wait for the train to come roaring through.

But now something else was on my mind. Commencement. Miss Lafayette had reminded us on Friday that it was coming up. I'd almost forgotten all about the eighth-grade ceremony commemorating the end of grammar school. Now I thought about the commencement dress Daddy's sister had sent from Chicago. White organza with a dropped pink sash. At first, I'd hung it on the back of the bedroom door, just so I could sit on my bed and look at it. But for the past few weeks I hadn't given that dress a thought or barely a look. Now, since Miss Lafayette put commencement back on my mind, I thought of Mama's rhinestone clip-on earrings.

"Mama," I said, hoping that she was going to grant my request.

"What is it?" She glanced over at me with annoyance.

"I was wonderin'—for my commencement, can I please wear them earrings Daddy sent you last fall?"

"My birthday earrings?"

"Please, Mama." I waited. She was squinting into the distance, actually thinking about it. That was a good sign, because when Mama said no right off, it was settled—as settled as could be.

"Okay," she said. Just like that. I couldn't believe it had been so easy. I kept my mouth closed, not wanting anything I said to change her mind.

"Thanks, Mama," was all I chanced a few moments later.

Miss Beach was on her porch, sipping her morning coffee and gliding gently back and forth. Treasure lay at her feet, his eyes closed to slits. I did not like that cat.

Miss Beach nodded good morning to us.

I started around back.

Before I could get down the stairs good, Miss Beach was asking me, "Were you up there meddling?"

"No, ma'am." I'd hoped to see Miss Lafayette. She'd made me feel better about Jesse's departure, telling me he'd probably be back—as soon as his farm workload lightened up. But her room was empty and there was no sign of her.

I dropped the laundry on the floor, then squatted down to sort it. Miss Beach stood over me for a minute, giving me the usual instructions. Finally, she left the room. I loaded my arms with the whites and took them out to Mama.

"Miss Beach wants these to go through two boiling tubs, Mama," I said, relaying Miss Beach's instructions.

Mama sighed. "If I don't know that by now, I must be a dimwit."

I smiled and then remembered the nickel I had in my pocket. I could taste the Scooter Pie I was going to buy with it as soon as I could get over to Green's. I just needed to get to my hill in time to see the local race by on its way up to Birmingham to make its connection to the Illinois Central. I loved watching that train. I was gonna be taking that route one day, on my way to Chicago. Daddy had promised.

Things went off without a hitch. Mama and I wrung and wrung the sheets, we hung the wash, and Miss Beach stayed out of our way. That horrid cat kept out of our way, too. Mama finally said I could go.

"You be home by the time I get there, missy," Mama said.

I quickly calculated that I'd have less time than I was counting on, but I was in such a good mood that it gave me only a pinprick of disappointment. I could make that up if I ran all the way to Green's.

I stopped at our house. Prez was gone down to Perry's. Good, I thought. He won't be pestering me to let him come along. I quickly went to get the *Nancy Drew* I was in the middle of reading.

I kept all my books on a little shelf above me and Mama's bed. She kept her earrings up there in a little box. I had to keep my books away from Prez. He liked to thumb through the pages and pick out the words he knew, his dirty hands smudging my pages. Miss Lafayette had given me a beautiful feather, dyed shocking pink, from an old hat, to use as a bookmark. I loved it. I always left it on my shelf to keep from losing it when I took a book out of the house.

"Page 58," I said to myself as I slipped the feather from between the pages and placed it carefully on the shelf.

Green's was nearly empty. Good, I thought. I wouldn't have to wait while white folks were helped before me.

"Hey, Francie," Vell said, coming out from the back and heading for the porch with a broom. He was Mr. Green's retarded nephew.

"Hey, Vell." I went directly to the counter where Scooter Pies were kept in their own display box. The box was empty. There was the jar of penny candy but no Scooter Pies. I checked every inch of the counter. The big jar of pickles—the jar of pickled eggs—no Scooter Pies. Naw, I thought. Couldn't be. Mr. Green sat behind the register, reading his paper and smoking his Old Gold. He flicked an ash into a jar lid.

"Mr. Green," I said politely. He looked up. "Don't you have any Scooter Pies?"

"You see any Scooter Pies, Francie?"

"No, sir."

He went back to his paper. "Then I don't have any. We're out."

I searched the counter again. It wasn't that I didn't believe him—I just had to be sure. Fingering my smooth nickel in my pocket, I walked to the porch and looked up the road toward town. I hadn't gotten permission to go there, though.

I knew Diller's Drugs would have Scooter Pies. A stack of them by the register. Sitting on my hill waiting on the local wouldn't be the same if I didn't have one to nibble on.

I skipped down the porch steps and headed for town. I tucked my book under my arm and put a little bounce in my step, determined to stay happy.

Diller's was empty enough, so I decided to look around a couple of minutes before I got my Scooter Pie. Mr. Diller was putting new magazines in the rack and taking out the old ones.

Eugene and Jimmy Early were sitting cross-legged on the floor, reading *Buck Rogers* comics.

"Excuse me," I said, trying to get around them, and when they ignored me and I had to squeeze past, one laughed. Then I felt something hit my back. It was a piece of wadded paper. I looked back at the boys. They held their comic books an inch from their noses, pretending innocence.

I went on my way, turning down the cosmetics aisle. Lined up on the shelves were creamy lotions and bath salts in the most wonderful colors. I sniffed at a closed bottle of cologne, too afraid to take the top off. I was careful to put it back exactly as I'd found it. There were pretty tortoiseshell combs and hairnets in all colors. I wished I could get one for Mama. She would like that.

I heard giggling behind me and turned to see Clarissa Montgomery, Verdie Johnson, and Holly Grace arriving at the lunch counter. I knew from overhearing Clarissa talking with her friends that they were giggling at Mr. Diller's son Joe. He'd just come home from the army and was working at the drugstore. Verdie and Clarissa reached for menus, but Holly slid off her stool and went over to the carousel that held all the copies of *Nancy Drew* and *Hardy Boys* and *Bobbsey Twins.* She gave it a twirl and withdrew one volume.

I made my way to the front for my Scooter Pie.

I took one from the display, set it carefully on the counter, then waited for Mr. Diller to finish writing things in what looked like a ledger. Finally, with a sigh, he ambled over to me.

"Eighty cents," Mr. Diller said.

"Pardon me?" I thought I hadn't heard right.

"Eighty cents," he repeated and tapped the counter with his nails.

I looked at my Scooter Pie. I wanted it—but not for

eighty cents. Maybe it was a price just for me. Maybe he aimed to keep colored out of his store. Whyn't he just put up a sign? I felt everyone watching me, hoping something was about to spice up their dull afternoon.

I thought about my words carefully, as I was accustomed to doing. "Sir, I was thinking Scooter Pies were a nickel." I avoided Mr. Diller's eyes.

"Yea, but that *Nancy Drew* you got tucked under your arm so's I can't see it . . ." He reached over and snatched it from under my arm and slapped it on the counter. "That there is seventy-five cents." He laid his meaty hand on top of it like a weight. There was no way I'd reach across that counter and try to remove that big hairy hand off my book.

I heard snickers coming from two directions. Holly and Verdie had turned on their stools and were grinning ear to ear. Clarissa's face showed no expression. She kept her head down and sipped on her soda, as if she didn't want to see what was happening.

I looked back at Eugene and Jimmy Early's stupid faces. "I didn't get that book from your store, Mr. Diller. I had it when I come in."

He squinted at it then. He removed his hand, picked the book up, and held it out in front of him, his eyes darting to his audience at the lunch counter. He turned the book this way and that.

"You trying to tell me you brought this book in with you?"

"Yes, sir. *The Secret of the Old Clock.* That's the truth."

"Why, it looks brand-new to me." He held it up to show the Early boys. "Don't it to you boys?"

"I think she stole that book," Jimmy Early piped up.

"She ain't had no book. I seen her come in empty-handed," Eugene said with scorn.

I met his eyes squarely. He blushed red with his lie. Jimmy kept his mouth shut, unwilling to get too bad a mark on his soul.

"He's lying on me, Mr. Diller."

"Is he, now?"

"Yes, sir."

Eugene, I guess believing his lie by now, stared back. "Mr. Diller, I seen her come in empty-handed. That's the truth." He inched toward me, but Mr. Diller put up his hand.

Holly had slid off her stool and come up for a closer gander, still sipping on her soda.

"Let me get this straight. You calling Eugene here a lie?" Mr. Diller asked.

I felt the trap he was laying for me. How could a colored call a white a lie?

"I'm saying I brought that book in here with me."

Mr. Diller came from around the counter and with a purposeful stride went right over to the carousel, counted the copies of *Nancy Drew*, and glanced back at me like I was cow manure.

"I just ten minutes ago put five new copies on that

carousel. I had five already, and that makes ten! Guess how many I got now?"

I said nothing, because in the middle of his counting—and he made quite a show of it—I knew there'd be one missing. He'd be short one, because Holly took it.

"Cat got your tongue?"

"No, sir."

"You want to guess, then?"

"No, sir." I looked directly at Holly. She gazed back at me level and confident.

"I got nine," he said, coming down hard on *nine.* He glanced around at the onlookers—from one to the other. "I got *nine.*" He seemed to be speaking only to them, like he was expecting them to bear witness.

I turned to Eugene. "You saw me take a book off that carousel?"

"I sure did," he said quickly.

"Did you see me with your own eyes?"

He seemed not to know how to answer that. Then: "Yea, I did."

"What I do with it?"

"Put it under your arm."

"I didn't open it and read it?"

"No, you just hid it under your arm and went right up to the register," he said.

"Okay." I turned back to Mr. Diller. "If you open up that book to page 58 you'll probably see a bit of pink feather in the binding. I use a feather as a bookmark, but I left it at home cause I didn't want to lose it."

He studied my face, then the book in his hand. He flipped to page 58. The bit of pink feather stood out on the page for everyone to see. Mr. Diller blew on it and it floated to the floor.

"Where's that missing book, then?" Eugene said.

I answered, just as calm as you please—though I don't know what could have prompted me to say such a thing—"Whyn't you all ask Holly. I seen her steal lipstick right off that display not too long ago." I pointed to the cosmetics aisle. "Maybe if you searched her purse . . ." I could hardly get the words out, she came at me so fast, jaws clenched.

"How dare you, you little pickaninny," she sputtered, enraged. Her slap sent my head spinning. She went to hit me again, and I ducked in time, so that her hand glanced off the back of my head, the palm side of her fingers connecting in a way that was probably more painful for her than me. Still, I actually saw little exploding lights in front of my open eyes. The place on my cheek where her hand had made contact had a fierce ringing sting. If I hadn't been dark, I figured I'd be wearing her palm print for days. "You want to stand there, you little black pickaninny, and call me a thief?"

Her face was as red as mine would have been if it could show. She reared back to strike me again, but Mr. Diller caught her hand.

"That ain't necessary, Holly." Joe Diller, who'd been in the back room, came out now to stop the ruckus. "Let me take care of this." He turned to me. "You get on out of here, and don't let me see you set foot in Diller's Drugs again."

I looked at my book in Mr. Diller's hand. My eyes started to fill with tears, but I willed them away. That man knew in his heart that the book belonged to me. But he was gonna stand there and act like I'd done something wrong, just to save face. I didn't understand white folks sometimes. I'd be too scared to be so mean.

I stepped out into the bright sunshine, which now seemed to mock my earlier good feeling. I was innocent, but the world had decided to make me guilty. Why did I feel so guilty? I walked toward my hill.

The ground trembled beneath me. I could hear the distant rumble of the train. I gazed in its direction as it came at me. I stood and waved at it. I was going to be on that train one day. I was going to get out of Alabama, God willing.

Commencement

On Monday, after the flag salute, after roll was called, after Miss Lafayette wrote down the problem of the day on the board and we grabbed our slates to start working it, she turned around and said, "Put your slates down for a moment."

She gazed around the room and then settled on our eighth-grade section, though all had to listen.

In her soft voice she began. "Now, you know, the end of the school year is right around the corner. Commencement is at the end of the month. Y'all will be going on to Thomas Jefferson." She stopped and closed her eyes. "I so much want you to use every opportunity that comes your way. There are scholarships to our Negro colleges and any one of you can get one of those scholarships and go on to become a teacher, or a lawyer, or a doctor even." She stopped and searched our faces. Already I felt a little buzz of excitement in the pit of my stomach. Even though I wouldn't be going to Thomas Jefferson, and didn't know where I'd be going up in Chicago. I just loved the thought of *possibilities.* It could almost make me forget Diller's on Saturday and everything I'd experienced like it.

Just as we started our lunches, Miss Lafayette called Augustine over to her desk, and we all guessed why. Augustine's sad expression as she walked out of the classroom and went straight into the woods served as proof.

"She knows she's gonna be held back," Serena said.

"Yea, she knows," I added, feeling a strange new sympathy for Augustine.

She didn't come back the rest of the day. The next morning she sheepishly entered the classroom with welts all up and down the back of her legs. Miss Lafayette didn't scold her for skipping out on school, and I knew she wouldn't. She just gave her a sympathetic smile. One of Augustine's little brothers or sisters must have told their daddy on her. Whatever the case, the wind seemed to be out of her sails. She hardly gave me a glance. For the rest of the day, when I saw her hunched over an arithmetic problem or mouthing words during silent reading time, a knot formed in my throat. Poor Augustine Butler. God had blessed me with knowing I could fight my way out of my circumstances, if need be. But she didn't know that like I did. No wonder she was so mean.

"Jesse's over at the Early farm, helping with the planting," Prez said two days later when he got home from working after school at the Early farm.

I stopped in my tracks. "You seen him there?"

"This very day."

"Jesse?"

"I said he's there."

"What'd he say?"

"He didn't say nothin'."

"He didn't ask about me?"

"What for?"

I shrugged. I didn't know what for.

For the rest of the evening, I thought about Jesse working over at the Early farm.

"Turn," Mama said to me, a spray of pins clenched in her teeth. I turned. "Not that much." I turned a bit the other way. "Stop. Hold still."

I nearly held my breath. She was hemming the white organza and taking a long time. A free Saturday—Miss Beach was down in Mobile and had told us to skip this day, since she wouldn't be there to supervise. I'd arranged to take a lunch to Prez and Perry. I wanted to see Jesse. But for now I was stuck standing uncomfortably on a kitchen chair.

"I just don't know . . ." Mama muttered to herself.

"When can I get down, Mama?"

"Not till I'm done."

She wasn't done until a half hour more of pinning, frowning, taking it out. As soon as she was satisfied, I hopped down, changed back into my regular clothes, grabbed the lunch pails, and ran out the door.

When Prez and Perry saw me, they dropped their hoes and left them lying on the ground. Prez looked back over his shoulder to see what Mr. Early's boss man Bellamy was doing. He was walking to the woods.

I held up the buckets and they made their way over.

"Why'd you take so long? We done missed our dinnertime," Prez whined.

"Now we'll have to work and eat at the same time," Perry said, his mouth in a pout.

"Mama held me up, hemming my dress." I set the buckets down. "Where's Jesse?"

"Bellamy has him cutting some wood," Prez said. He pulled up a drooping overall strap.

Jesse just then came out of the woods, carrying a stack of logs. I had to resist the urge to shout his name. He dumped them on the edge of the field and went back.

"Jesse ain't got time for company," Perry said. "He been in trouble already. Bellamy pretendin' Jesse's not workin' fast enough for his size. He lookin' to cut his pay."

"That ain't fair."

"Betcha he gon' do it."

Jesse came out with another load, his head down. I waved anyway, but he went back into the woods without looking up.

Miss Lattimore mopped her forehead in the hot sun and began reading from her notes. Commencement day had finally arrived. We'd rehearsed the way we'd shake with one hand and take our diploma with the other, all week. Already sweat was running down my neck and making my dress stick to my back. But I didn't mind. Here I was, wearing Mama's earrings! I sat in the first row on our little makeshift stage: a thick piece of plywood on bricks. Serena, in her homemade dress of beige muslin, sat beside me. A mosquito landed on my arm and I swatted at it just in time.

Mama sat in the second row in the swept school yard, next to Aunt Lydia, who had suddenly seemed to blow up even bigger with child. Perry, in clean, pressed overalls, sat next to her, then Uncle June in his black going-to-meeting suit. Prez wore new dungarees Daddy had sent him and a white shirt. Perry and Prez would be going up to Benson with Uncle June later that evening for a week-long visit. Uncle June had been there working in a turpentine factory, planning to move his family after Auntie had her baby.

Auntie had told Mama she looked forward to the quiet

not having Perry underfoot would bring. I looked forward to the peace as well.

Miss Lattimore's voice lifted to reach the back rows. Prez squirmed and ran a finger around his collar to loosen it. Mama began to fan. Miss Lafayette looked over at me from the side of our stage and smiled. Finally, Miss Lattimore got to the last page of her notes and with another mop of her face sat down.

It was time for Miss Lafayette to give out the awards. Serena got the penmanship award. J. Dean got the attendance. I got the award for academic achievement. When Miss Lafayette handed me my certificate in my left hand and reached out to shake my right, I could have floated right up into the clouds. Mama beamed. She was proud. A smile was all I was going to get, but I didn't care. I knew what was in her heart and mind, and her smile was worth more than gold.

Sunday at the Montgomerys'

"You're going to have to go to Mrs. Montgomery's, Francie, and start those cakes." Mama adjusted her hat in front of the little cracked mirror hanging over the basin stand where we washed our faces. "I'll be down the street at Mrs. Grace's, since I promised I'd get her floors waxed for her book-club meeting tonight."

My heart sank at the memory of Holly Grace and the sting of her slap. I hoped Mama wouldn't find out about it. Mama took her hat off and hit it against her thigh, then set it on her head again and twisted it a bit. She frowned at herself in the mirror. "When we get up to Chicago, I'm sure getting me a brand-new town hat—I'm so sick of this one."

She turned to me. "Okay, as soon as you get to Mrs.

Montgomery's, start on the icing. I want it nice and chilled by the time I get there. You can go on and make the cakes, so they can cool, too. You listening to me?"

"Yes, ma'am."

All the way to Mrs. Montgomery's I dreaded the thought of seeing that priss, Clarissa. Maybe she'd gone back home to Baltimore. I hoped.

"I'm on the phone," Mrs. Montgomery told me as she let me in the back door. She hurried out of the room, leaving me standing there in her cool, spotless kitchen. "Help yourself to the radio," she called.

I started setting out all the things I was going to need. I had two kinds of sheet cake to make, with three kinds of icing, and if Mama was really late, I'd have to cut the cakes into diamonds and hearts and squares like Mrs. Montgomery always wanted for her teas, with cherries on some and nuts on the others.

"Stay out of them nuts, Francie," Mama had warned. "I know how you like to nibble as you go."

I found the jar of pecans in the cupboard, opened it, and popped one in my mouth. Pausing at the window, I noticed someone fixing the busted bottom step on the backyard gazebo. I reached for another pecan. There was something familiar about that man, though I couldn't see his face. I screwed the lid back on the jar and set it down.

The morning sun was warm on my shoulders as I

headed across the lawn. I don't think he even heard me coming. I walked over to him and looked down. "Hey, Jesse."

He squinted up at me. "Hey, Francie."

"Been wondering what happened to you."

"Workin' here and there." He reached for a nail.

"You left and never came back."

"I couldn't. I had to help my daddy with the late plantin'."

"We had our commencement."

"I wouldn't have been part of no commencement, no-how." I saw the tiny hurt in his eyes.

"You were learning pretty fast."

He looked down at the hammer in his hand. "No mind."

I asked carefully, "You still reading?"

"Some." He fiddled with his hammer.

"You going to school, *ever* again?"

"Ain't got time for school. I gotta work. My daddy run off and it's just me."

That stopped me. I'd heard of people's daddies running off. My daddy wasn't around, but he sure hadn't run off.

"What about your brother and sister?"

"They with relatives."

I didn't know what to say.

"I better go, Jesse."

He nodded and I headed back to the house.

. . .

"You got everything you need," Mrs. Montgomery said, eyeing the table.

"I believe I do."

She pursed her mouth. "Okay, I'll leave you to your work."

As I worked, I listened to *Homemaker's Exchange* on the radio. A lady was discussing the three danger zones of a woman's face—under eye, nose, and throat—and the wonderful rejuvenating qualities of Dorothy Gray emollient.

I'd just started measuring out the flour for the first cake when a voice from behind me said, "Hi." I turned around and there was Clarissa Montgomery standing in the kitchen doorway, her hands behind her back.

"Hey," I answered, turning to face her. I waited.

"What are you doing?"

"Making cakes."

"You know how to make a cake?"

Was she funning me? Who couldn't make a cake? "Yea," I answered. She moved into the room and I stiffened, neither of us saying a word. Finally, she held something out to me.

I stared down at my book. My *Nancy Drew—The Secret of the Old Clock.* She laid it on the table. "I bought it—but it was always yours."

I felt my face grow hot, remembering the shame of being accused though innocent. I hadn't even confided that horrible incident to Serena. Now I found my voice and said, "I wouldn't steal no book. My teacher gave me that book."

"I believe you." She didn't explain why she didn't come to my defense, and I didn't care to ask her about it. I never expect a white to take up for me, anyway. I was mostly glad to get my book back.

"Thank you."

Clarissa sat down. I started in on my work, trying to ignore her.

"I was waiting to give that book to you."

"I appreciate it," I said again and continued working.

She watched in silence for a moment. "What's that?" she asked.

I looked at the object in my hand. "A sifter."

"What's it for?"

"For *sifting.*"

"What's sifting?"

How could she not know about sifting? "Mixing stuff together and making them powdery," I said. I handed her the sifter. "Here. I'll let you do it some."

She took it and began to squeeze the handle. "You have to hit the side with the palm of your hand from time to time." She hit it and I sat down.

"That boy outside," I started. "How long has he been working for you all?"

"Jesse Pruitt? Awhile," Clarissa answered. "Aunt Myra hired him to get the gazebo ready for her outdoor brunch coming up." She switched hands.

"I used to tutor him," I said, not knowing why.

"Oh?" She looked toward the window. "In what?"

"I was teaching him to read."

"Didn't he know how to read?" She stopped and shook her hand. "My hand hurts."

"Not much." I picked up the sifter and took up where she left off.

Suddenly she looked over at the stove clock. "Oh no! I'm supposed to be dressed. Aunt Myra's going to kill me." She was gone in a flash.

The cakes were in the oven, the icing was in the refrigerator, and I was alone with my thoughts. I swished my hand in the warm sudsy water in the sink and began washing the dishes, so they wouldn't pile up.

Suddenly Clarissa was back and standing in the doorway, shyly holding another book. "Please give this to Jesse. Aunt Myra has all of Cousin Victor's books still up in his old room and I found this one." She held out the book. "He's been gone to college for two years now. Don't think he's still interested in books he read as a kid."

It was a copy of *Aesop's Fables*. Miss Lafayette had lent me that book last spring and I'd read every one of them fables. Jesse would like it. I dried my hands and took the book. I opened it. The stories were short, I was reminded, and simple.

"He can have it?"

"Why not? Auntie was getting ready to donate it to the library fund-raiser, anyway."

I looked out the window, imagining Jesse bent over his work, sweating in the hot sun.

"Thank you," I said. "I know he'll be happy to have it."

She left me alone then. I went back to work on the dirty dishes.

Mama didn't get there until after one. "Mrs. Grace had me do some *light* ironing," she said. "I couldn't refuse." She looked over at the iced cakes and sighed. She tied on an apron and went to the sink to wash her hands. She kind of moved me over with her hip and went to work, pulling crusts off bread for the finger sandwiches, chopping onion for the salmon mold. I watched, then wandered over to the window to check on Jesse, but I didn't see him. The step looked finished, except for needing paint. Jesse was probably in the work shed right then, mixing some.

Mama started to sing "Sweet By and By," which meant she was already lost in her work. I could disappear for a few minutes. I slipped out the door and across the yard, around to the shed. It was padlocked. I'd been all prepared to see his smile when I gave him the book, and now I was too late. He'd already gone. I felt like I was in a deep pit. The kind you drop down into from a place of high hopes.

"Mama, Clarissa Montgomery did something nice for me." We were walking home in the late afternoon.

"Mmm." Mama was tired and she didn't talk much

when she was tired. But I wasn't feeling tired at all. I wanted to tell Mama the whole story, but I couldn't. I'd get myself into trouble for going into town without permission and for tutoring Jesse instead of coming straight home every day. "That was good of her."

"That's what I was thinking."

Then Mama looked me over, narrowing her eyes. "Don't you be too fooled by that. I've seen 'em friendly one minute and turn just as fast the next. Depending on their mood."

I'd seen the same thing. Soon as you began counting on white folks to be one way, they'd remind you of your place. I didn't care. I had my book back.

The sun was sinking behind the trees and Mama and me were walking step-in-step and I was feeling satisfied. How was I going to get *Aesop's Fables* to Jesse? Mentally, I made a list right then of all the books I wanted him to read. Miss Lafayette would help me find a way to keep teaching him. I only had to convince Jesse. We'd take him on as our project. He was motherless and fatherless. He was without even his little brother and sister. I knew Miss Lafayette felt nearly as sorry for him as I did.

Janie Arrives

Janie's early arrival spiced things up a bit. We were expecting her at the end of the month, but in early June, long after everyone had been good and asleep, there was a banging on the door. I sat up with a start and Mama jumped out of bed and ran around, trying to find her robe. "Auntie's time must be here," she said.

Prez beat me to the door, letting in the night air and the hum of crickets. Perry stepped in.

"Mama's getting ready to have her baby," he said. "You gotta come now, Aunt Lil."

"Sure, baby." Mama looked over at Prez. "You and Perry run down and get Granny." Granny was the midwife. She delivered everybody's baby.

"Can I come, Mama?"

Mama looked me over, calculating if I was old enough. "For a little bit," she said, not wanting to promise more. Then we were out the door, rushing up the road toward Auntie's in the pitch-black night, with only a lantern lighting the way.

The gravelly crunch of our hurrying feet seemed loud in the still night. I had thrown on Daddy's big nightshirt over my gown. I ran after Mama, who was taking huge strides. All the way there, I thought: No Miss Beach, this day.

As we stepped into the house, we could hear groans coming from the back room. Auntie Lydia was rolling around on her bed in pain. I stopped short and stared.

"Stop, Lydia," Mama scolded. "You know rolling around makes it worse."

Auntie just raised her pitiful face to Mama and there were tears in her eyes. "I can't do this," she said.

"Don't be silly. You ain't got no choice in the matter." Mama sat down and helped her turn over on her side. "Breathe slow," she said, rubbing Auntie's back.

"I can't."

"Come on, now. You done it before."

"I can't," she cried, and the cry rose up, ending with a gasp. She shrieked as if the pain surprised her.

"That makes it worse, Lydia," Mama said. But Auntie just began to writhe again, moaning, her face covered in beads of sweat.

Mama found a rag and threw it to me. "Go outside and

wet this at the pump. Then wring it out and bring it back."

I hurried out onto the dark porch, pausing there a moment, blind in the moonless night. I had to feel for the pump. It took four or five good pumps before cool water began to flow. I held the rag under it for a while, wrung it, and turned to go inside.

At the same time, something rustled nearby. A small crackling sound that cut off sharp, not dying away as if it was all in innocence. I squinted in its direction. All was suddenly too still, a silence filled with guilt. I waited, listening. Nothing. A possum maybe, scrounging for food.

Quickly, I made my way to the bedroom with the wet rag. Mama took it and dabbed at Auntie's forehead. Auntie clutched at her hand. "How far apart are your pains, Lydia?" Mama asked her.

"Every time I catch my breath, seem like." The next wave hit her, in answer, and Auntie rolled away from Mama and began to groan miserably.

Mama checked the door, her brow frozen in a worried line. I knew she was hoping to see Granny there. "I sent Prez and Perry to get Granny. She should be here any minute." Mama loosened Auntie's grip and helped her lie back to rest in the space between pains.

Granny came through the door then. "Here I am," she said. Mama sighed. "I sent Prez and Perry on to your place, Lil." Wearing her faded kerchief, long loose dress, and apron with deep pockets that held all sorts of necessities, Granny hurried into the room, carrying a washbasin and a cloth bag. From it she pulled a sheet, a square of quilted material, and an ax. She handed the ax to me. "Here, missy. Slip this under the bed to cut the after-pains. Lift your hips, Lydia." Granny helped Auntie while positioning the quilted square under her. Then she clapped her hands once. "Help me tie the ends of this sheet"—she held out the sheet to me—"to the bedposts. This poor chile's gonna need something to pull on." After I had tied the ends in place, she asked me, "Are they good and tight?"

I pulled at them. "Yes, ma'am."

"Good. Go on, now. We ain't gonna need you around here. Go tend to your little brother and cousin."

Mama nodded in agreement. Granny was in charge now.

Disappointed, I left Auntie's and stepped out into the weak, milky light of early morning. More time had passed than I'd thought. A thin fog had settled across the fields and road, blurring every sharp edge. In the new light I scanned the overgrown shrubbery by the side of the house, where I'd heard the strange rustling. Nothing. I searched the road and the fields, looking in the direction of the woods. Nothing. It must have been a possum making that noise, like I thought.

I walked home slowly, wondering about childbirth and why it had to hurt so much. Prez and Perry were already asleep when I got back. I was glad to crawl into bed, but it felt empty without Mama next to me.

I fell into a deep sleep.

Mama stayed down to Auntie's and let Prez and Perry and me sleep in. It felt good to wake up in my own time—and with a happy thought of a brand-new baby. I hurried into my clothes, threw some water on my face, and rushed down the road to Auntie's. Mama met me at her door.

"Shhh. Auntie and the baby are asleep."

"What'd she have, Mama?"

"A girl." Mama smiled. "She named her Janie."

"Janie."

"You go on home and come down later. I want you to write to Uncle June and tell him the news and that everybody's fine. Then you'll need to stop by Mrs. Beach's and tell her why we ain't comin' today." Mama reached into her pocket. "Here." She put some money in my hand. "Go by Green's, too, and get me a pound of coffee. You can get yourself and Prez a Scooter Pie. I'ma be down here awhile."

I looked at the money. It was like a ticket to heaven. I had a free day.

Granny stopped by our house a little later, after Perry went back home, to tell us about the baby. Janie had come fast when she decided to make her appearance, hollering right away.

"I'ma need a cup of tea, Francie," she said to me. "Some black cohosh if you have any."

Later, she sat there sipping away while she filled me and Prez in on everything. She leaned back and squinted her eyes. "Let me tell you. That baby's going to be something, being born between the two lights like she was." Daybreak and sunrise, she meant.

Granny believed a host of superstitions. Mama hated superstition, so I had a little guilty thrill sitting there listening to her. "Betcha she ain't gonna have no problem making it to her second birthday. You watch."

I hoped Granny would get started telling me some stories about haints and ghosts. She slept with a fork under her pillow, and when the "witches rode her," she slept with a sifter under her bed, so they'd have to go through every hole before they could bother her. I wanted to hear the story about her waking up to see a haint sitting right on the foot of her bed watching her sleep. That gave me nightmares the first time she told me.

"That's pure ignorance," Mama always said when I asked her about such. "Just some old stuff from slavery times." I waited, but Granny wasn't up to her stories this morning. She was so tired she started to doze right there over her tea.

Scooter Pie . . . at Last!

After Granny left, Prez went down to Perry's to see if he wanted to go fishing, and I wrote a short letter to Uncle June, put a stamp on it, and left it in our mailbox. Then I walked over to Miss Beach's, then to Green's to get Mama's coffee and me and Prez Scooter Pies. Mama always bought Chase & Sanborn. I put the can of coffee and the Scooter Pies on the counter, but no one was around, not even Vell. Finally, he came shuffling out of the storeroom, carrying a box of canned goods.

"Where's Mr. Green?" I asked.

"Out back, talkin' to some men."

"Well, I want to buy this coffee and these Scooter Pies." I jingled the money in my pocket and looked at my treat with longing. "Can you go get him?"

"Naw."

"Why?"

He looked down, embarrassed like he didn't know what to say. "He's back there with them other men and they're talking like they're mad."

"About what?"

"I ain't gonna go interruptin' them, neither."

"Well, can you take the money for these?"

I put the money on the counter. He looked at it. "I better not," he said.

"Come on, Vell. Mr. Green won't mind."

"He might get mad."

"Not if you get the right amount."

He pinched his lips together, thinking.

"He ain't gonna get mad, Vell." I pushed the money toward him. He stepped back like he was afraid of it. Then he slapped his hand down over it quick. I grabbed my coffee and Scooter Pies just as fast, before he could change his mind.

I dropped the coffee off, set Prez's Scooter Pie on our table, fetched my *Nancy Drew*, and made it to my hill with time to spare. The sun was scorching. In the direction the train would approach, all was still, like nothing moving was ever going to come that way. The tracks, shimmering a gleaming silver, wound out of sight where the woods met the gully running next to the tracks' incline. I pushed my bare feet into the cool grass and slowly tore the cellophane wrapper off my Scooter Pie. Once all of it was off, I held the pie up and turned it slowly, studying it with anticipation. I scraped a bit of the hard chocolate frosting on the edge of my teeth and let it melt on my tongue. I had my book once again and my pie—I was happy.

Just then I heard someone singing behind me, at the bottom of the hill—riverside. I could hear a banjo, too. I crept to the other side of the hill and lay flat on my stomach. There was a hobo camp down by the river—by the viaduct. I knew about hoboes. Sometimes one would come to the door for a handout, and if Mama thought he was harmless, she'd hand him out a sweet potato or some hot-water corn bread.

There were about six or seven of them, both black and white. Someone had built a lean-to out of an old packing crate, and two men were cooking some food over a fire right in front of it. The music was coming from the one sitting by the river's edge. He was singing along with his banjo and then he closed his mouth and let his fingers fly, making a lively tune, making himself feel good, I guess—for a time. I was blessed to have picked just this time to watch for my train. It was almost as good as a picture show, looking at them. One was mending a shirt, another tying his bedroll, and there was another sitting on a flat rock just staring out at the water. Probably thinking about what a miserable turn his life had taken.

The lonely little figure who'd been gazing out at the

river stood up. Something strange about that one, but I couldn't put my finger on it. He began to climb the hill in my direction. When he drew closer, I saw that he wasn't a *he* at all. He was a *she*—dressed in men's clothes. She had a sharp birdlike face, with sad, startled eyes. She was colored, caramel skin. Adjusting the man's cap, she turned and shaded her eyes in my direction. She clutched a lumpy satchel like she wasn't ever gonna let it go.

I sat up and let myself be seen. She jumped a little and stopped in her tracks.

"Hey, you," she called out. "What you doin'?" She climbed closer, grabbing at a bush with her free hand to pull herself up.

She came right up to me and squatted down. She set her bag in front of her and looked at it as if measuring whether it was safe so close to a stranger. She was skinnier than I'd thought, her arms wiry and ropy with veins. Her lean face, all sharp chin and cheekbones, showed that she was older, as well. As old as twenty-five, maybe.

"What's your name?" she asked.

"Francie."

"My name's Alberta—after my daddy."

"Alberta . . . There was a character named Alberta in a book I read once."

She studied my face to see if I was lying, it seemed. Then she shoved some stray hair back under her cap. "You read?" she said.

"Course."

Her mouth flicked down at the corners like Prez's when he was trying not to cry. But she recovered quickly and said, "I never got to go to school."

"Why?"

"Never mind."

She sat there silent for a while. I kept quiet too. Her eyes dropped to my Scooter Pie with the one bite out of it and I saw her swallow.

"You hungry?"

"Naw."

"Me neither. Here, take my Scooter Pie." Mama had told me you shouldn't ever let someone go hungry if you had something to share. It was sinful.

She shrugged and took it. She ate it quickly, almost choking on it. She licked the inside of the wrapper. "I came up here to look for some place—away from them mens—to go to the bathroom."

"Do they know you're a girl?"

"I don't know. I keep to myself and they don't bother me none." She licked her fingers.

"You traveling with them?"

"I'm traveling on my own. I'm going to New Orleans, then hopping a freight out to California."

"California?"

"It seem like the place to go. Land of opportunity . . ." Her voice drifted off and she had that getting-ready-to-cry look again.

"Where are your people? Where's your folks?"

"Here and there."

I stared at her in wonder. Imagine traveling alone like that. Just picking a place and deciding to go.

She stood up and looked around. "I'ma go behind them bushes over yonder. You tell me if anybody be comin'." She slipped and slid down a bit of incline to a row of thick brush. Then she disappeared behind it. I checked the camp at the base of the hill again, deciding her privacy was safe.

Suddenly it was coming. The local heading to Birmingham . . . The ground trembled beneath me and a faint curl of white smoke plumed above the trees beyond where the tracks curved out of sight. It was coming! I could hear its whistle and that sh-sh-sh sound of steel wheels on steel track.

Finally, a thunderous roar brought that big black round face of the engine into view. I hadn't stood up good before it was racing by and I was counting cars and squinting at the windows to see the people in them. I waved and waved until it was out of sight.

"What you doin'?" Alberta said from behind me.

"Waving to my train."

She stood there with me looking down the empty tracks. "I do like trains," she said. "Cause they're full of possibility."

That was just how I felt. They took you to places of *possibility.*

Alberta started down the hill. Halfway, she turned

around and waved. I waved back. Although I wanted to see my new cousin, I wasn't ready to go home yet. I felt sleepy. I lay down, right there, and using my arms for a pillow, closed my eyes for a nap.

I dreamed someone was watching me—from the woods. Someone was standing there at its edge, just out of reach of the open light, staring at me. I woke with a start, whipped my head around in all directions, then sat there for a while barely breathing, listening as hard as I could. For what, I don't know.

I sighed, got up, brushed off the backside of my cotton dress, and started down the small hill toward the road, my bare soles relishing the places where the grass was slick and cool. I was going to see a new baby girl.

Clarissa's Room

"Want to see my room?" Clarissa said on Tuesday.

I couldn't look at no room. I had work to do. I wiped the sweat off my forehead with my apron. I was down on my knees, rolling up the heavy area rug in the living room. Me and Mama had come to wax the floors. "I can't," I said. "I gotta roll up the rugs."

"I can help you."

"No you can't, neither."

"Why?"

She looked funny with her sunburned face peeling across the nose, her face round and plain as the moon. Her pink shirred sundress showed off red shoulders.

"Cause my mama wouldn't like it. Your aunt neither."

"Well, come up then, for just a bit."

I looked toward the dining room, where Mama was working. Maybe I could sneak up for just a little while.

"I was going to show you my books."

I looked toward the dining room again. I thought about them books.

"Okay," I said, standing quickly.

Clarissa led the way and I tiptoed up the stairs behind her, while she chattered on. "Aunt Myra decorated this room for me because she thought I needed cheering."

"Do you need cheering?" I asked. Such a thought was unknown to me. I couldn't remember anyone concerned with cheering me up.

"Not much anymore," Clarissa said, throwing open the door. Stepping aside, she allowed me to go in ahead of her. It was like something I'd never seen. One whole wall was nothing but bookshelves like a library. I'd never really been in a library, but when I moved to Chicago, I was going to find me one.

I cocked my head sideways and began to read the titles: some I'd read already, some I ain't never heard of. I'd read *Silas Marner* in seventh grade. And *David Copperfield* last winter.

Clarissa was pulling back her curtains over a window seat covered in the same fabric. "I picked this fabric myself. Aunt Myra and I got it in Mobile."

It *was* pretty. I liked cornflowers. What was it like to wake up in a room like this every morning, I wondered. I pictured myself sitting in the gazebo on a summer evening, with a glass of lemonade with shaved ice and a good book.

"Can you keep a secret?" she asked suddenly.

"I guess . . ." I said slowly.

"First"—she squinted at me—"how old are you?"

"Almost thirteen." I already knew Clarissa was fourteen.

"Skinny little thing like you? Is your growth stunted?"

"Mama said I take after her people, small and wiry."

Clarissa seemed to consider this. "What grade you in?"

"I just had my eighth-grade commencement."

"And you ain't even thirteen yet?"

"I'll be thirteen soon—at the end of summer."

"I guess you're old enough to keep a secret."

She went to the bed, bent down, and pulled out a notebook from underneath. She patted the bed beside her. I crossed the room and sat down.

Her eyes were bright as she searched my face. "I'm writing a book."

"How you doing that?" I asked. I'd never heard of a person writing a book before, though I guessed someone had to.

"I'm writing a little each day. It's going to take me a long time, because I want it to be longer than *War and Peace.*" She stopped. "You've heard of that book?"

"I know it's real long. I haven't read it yet, though."

"So far, it's my favorite book. In fact, I've decided to name my first girl Natasha because of it."

“Natasha . . .” It sounded like a sneeze.

“My book is going to be better than *War and Peace*,” she said, like just uttering the words would make it so.

“My mama says it’s not nice to brag.”

“I’m not bragging if it’s true.”

“You can brag about things that are true.”

Suddenly Mama was calling up the stairs. I looked at Clarissa and hurried out to the landing. She came after me. And before I could look down into Mama’s angry face, Clarissa pushed a big, thick book in my hand. “I finished this a while ago. You can have it.”

I took it because I didn’t know what else to do. It was heavy in my hand. “Thanks,” I murmured before I rushed down the stairs to Mama’s scolding.

“Girl, if you don’t get your behind down here . . . You think Mrs. Montgomery is paying for you to visit with her niece?” I set the book on the hall table. Mama didn’t notice.

As I scooted by Mama to get back to the living room, she popped me on the head with her knuckle.

Just when I thought we were finished, after Clarissa had skipped out the door and down the walk with her friends, Mrs. Montgomery came into the kitchen, where Mama and I were putting away the cleaning supplies, and stood there wringing her hands and smiling.

“I hate to ask this, but can you two stay and polish the silver? I’ve got unexpected company coming tomorrow.”

She smiled and shrugged. I looked at Mama but Mama didn't meet my eyes.

"Course, Mrs. Montgomery. I'd be happy to. But I gotta send Francie on home so she can look in on Lydia. She just delivered a short while ago and still needs help."

"And the upstairs linen. I forgot to ask you to change it," Mrs. Montgomery said, as if her mind had never left her own concern.

"I'll get right on it." Mama turned and left the room. I went over and picked up the book Clarissa gave me. It was *War and Peace.*

Daddy's Coming

I went right over to Auntie's and spent the rest of the day cleaning and washing for her, so she wouldn't have anything to do but take care of Janie. Mama came by to pick me up and we were walking down Three Notch together when we noticed the flag was up on our mailbox. "Run over to the box and get our mail," Mama said, climbing the porch steps heavily.

We hadn't heard from Daddy in weeks. I pulled the single letter out of the box and immediately checked the postmark. Chicago. I marched the letter to Mama.

She took it out of my hand and leaned it against the sugar bowl on the table. She still had to wash her face.

"That from Daddy?" Prez asked, coming over to look at it.

"Yea, and don't you touch it."

Mama finally sat down. She picked up the letter, opened it, and held it for a moment. Then she handed it to me to read. I read it aloud word for word, then raced to reread the part about him coming home. Sunday. Four days from tomorrow. Mama took it back and looked at it. "Where does it say that?"

I pointed to the words. We all sat almost holding our breath and finding it hard to believe. It'd been over a year since Daddy had left us. He was tired of being without his family. When Mama said, "I'ma go on down and see how Auntie's doin'," I knew she was just trying to get away to hide her excitement. "You two go on and heat up the supper. We gonna have a lot to do between now and Sunday."

I knew what I was going to do. I was going to go buy Daddy a present. A pipe, God willing, because he'd look handsome smoking a pipe. I saw one at Green's, so I wouldn't even have to go into town to get it. I wouldn't have to go to the place I'd been practically run out of.

I woke up with a buzz of planning in my head early the next morning. I went to the outhouse and met Prez on the way. He'd already made his trip.

"Perry was just here. He said he came to get Mama at dawn. Auntie's not feeling well. She's sick. Mama wants you down there as soon as you can get dressed."

He looked smug with this news and I could have popped him. With Mama distracted with caretaking

Auntie, I knew he and Perry would be off to the fishing hole.

"What about you?"

"Me and Perry are workin' over at the Early farm today."

Mama probably had plans to use up most of my morning, but if I hurried I could get down to Green's by early afternoon.

Auntie had visitors. Nola Grandy and her daughter, Violet, were there with a potato pie and a bouquet of black-eyed Susans. Granny was there, having come with a sugar tit for Baby Janie and some catnip tea. She brought a chicken feather tied in red flannel for Auntie to hang around the baby's neck, but Mama had stepped in—taking it from Granny and dropping it in her pocket.

"I ain't puttin' that nasty thing around Baby Janie's sweet little neck," Mama whispered to me when Granny wasn't looking.

Auntie looked tired and pale and I knew Mama was worried about her getting childbirth fever. Women died from it all the time. Mama had tightly braided Auntie's hair into two thick cornrows that pulled her face to show her cheekbones. She looked pretty, but it was a tired pretty. Janie nursed at her breast.

Two loud knocks sounded on the front door. Before anyone could say anything, Miss Mabel stepped into the room.

"I'm comin' to see that new baby," she announced. She walked straight across the room to stare down at Janie. "My, that's a fine baby." She scooped Janie out of Auntie's arms just as Auntie was settling her after burping her. Before Auntie could protest, she carried Janie to the window.

"Mabel . . ." Mama said, standing.

"Aw, I ain't gonna steal her." She squinted at Janie. "Bright like her daddy's people." She lifted a tiny hand to the light. "But the rims around her fingers are pretty dark. She's gonna be brown." Mama and Auntie exchanged uneasy looks. "She got a whole lotta hair, I see. It's gonna be kinky."

Mama rescued Janie out of Miss Mabel's arms and returned her to Auntie. "You don't know that, Mabel."

"Yea, sure I do. Ain't that right, Granny? You seen a bunch of babies and how they turn out." Granny didn't answer, just sat there, arms crossed.

Miss Mabel got herself a comfortable seat at the table with the other women. "You heard about that boy they after."

"Sure did," said Nola.

Mama glanced over at me and gave a little quick nod that was meant to convey something to them. They all turned to stare at me then. I'd found a little corner to sit in, hoping to just sit and catch some grownup conversation, which was always interesting. "Go on, Francie, and get to washing them diapers," Mama said now. "Auntie's gonna need some before you know it."

"They offerin' a reward," Miss Mabel said as I walked out into the blistering-hot morning.

A pile of wet diapers and sheets sat at my feet. One by one, I pulled them out of the basket, shook them, and pinned them to the line. It had taken all morning to wash them, and now the sun beat ferociously on my back and biting flies were making mad dashes at my arms. The baby was sleeping peacefully and the company had gone home to start their dinners.

I grabbed a sheet and sunk my hot face into its cool, clean scent, almost missing a bright flash of red skirting the edge of the woods. If I'd blinked, I would have missed it. I squinted, staring at the place until I wondered if I'd imagined it. Just trees and undergrowth stared back. I finished hanging up the laundry, put the basket up against the porch, and skipped out of there. I had money from my can under the bed. I smiled, thinking of Daddy's pleasure when I gave him his present.

Run, Jesse, Run

Some white farmers stood just inside the door at Green's, huddled in conversation. When I squeezed by, they stopped talking until I passed. I found the rack of pipes. I chose a shiny black one with a white mouthpiece. At the register, Mr. Green leaned on the counter, picking his teeth with a toothpick and watching the group by the door.

I put my pipe on the counter. Mrs. Early came up then with boxes of Musterole and Triscuit Shredded Wheat. She set her items on the counter and with the back of her hand moved my item to the side.

I looked up at her sagging chin and limp hair the color of mud. She started up some talk with Mr. Green about the hot humid weather. I waited. I whistled "Camptown

Races." My eyes drifted to the wall behind the register. Something pasted up there made me stop dead.

It was a black-and-white "wanted" picture of Jesse Pruitt. My lips parted and my heart pounded and my hands shook. My mouth went dry. I nearly spoke his name: *Jesse . . .*

The photograph was hazy, as if it had been part of a group picture once and someone had cut out his face and made it bigger. But the straight brow and hesitant eyes were unmistakable. Under it were the words:

WANTED: *A colored boy who goes by the name of Jesse Pruitt for the attempted murder of Mr. Rosco Bellamy, the foreman for Mr. Robert Early. Use precaution. He is considered armed and dangerous. Reward offered.*

"What you starin' at, Francie?" Mr. Green asked me.

I looked down, feeling like I'd been caught stealing candy.

"Nothin', Mr. Green."

"You seen that boy?" he asked.

"No, sir," I was able to answer honestly.

"Well, if you do, you let me know directly, you hear?"

I said nothing.

"You hear me?" he said louder.

Mrs. Early narrowed her eyes at me, making her face ugly and mean. "What's wrong with you?" she asked.

"Nothing, ma'am."

"Then what's taking you so long to answer Mr. Green, here?"

"Yes, sir," I said quietly. Mrs. Early gathered up her purchases, dropped her change in her pocketbook, and snapped it shut.

"You takin' up smokin', Francie?" Mr. Green laughed at his own joke.

"It's for my daddy. He's comin' home on Sunday." I paid and stepped out onto the sidewalk in time to see Mrs. Early making her way across the road, where her husband was starting the engine of their car, his straw hat pushed to the back of his head and his fringe of hair plastered to his red forehead in dark sweaty points. He slowly scratched the back of his neck. I felt a deep abiding fear, watching after them.

He gunned the motor then, and they took off in a cloud of red dust.

"I know that boy," Vell said suddenly from behind me.

I whirled around.

"I seen him."

"Where, Vell?"

"I was out looking for my dog in the woods out by your place and I seen him. And he run from me." He paused and his lower lip drooped. "He didn't have to run from me. I wasn't after him."

I believed Vell. "You gonna tell?"

"Naw. Cause I know him and I like him."

"Don't tell—please." I felt I had to say it. "It's real important that you don't tell nobody, Vell, please. Please."

He looked insulted. "I told you I wasn't," he said and walked back toward the store.

When I got home, I did a few chores, then I waited on the porch for Prez. Juniper slept at my feet, twitching through a dream. Prez wouldn't be getting back from the Early farm until the sun was nearly touching the trees.

Finally, I could see two little figures making their way up the road. I got up and began to pace. They seemed to be taking so long I ran to meet them.

"When was the last time you seen Jesse?" I said, starting right in.

Prez shrugged his thin little shoulders. I looked to Perry. "Jesse's in trouble," he said.

"When you seen him last?" I repeated.

"Before we went up to Benson visiting Uncle June," Prez said. "Now everybody after him, sayin' he tried to kill Mr. Bellamy." Prez looked like he was going to cry. "Are they gonna catch him, Francie?"

I didn't answer. I didn't want to think about it.

I turned away and walked slowly back up the road to our house. I had supper to get on.

Jesse filled my mind—so much so I couldn't get to sleep that night, and when morning came, I couldn't tell if I'd done more than doze. I'd talked Mama's ear off with my fears and suspicions that he was hiding out nearby, until she turned over and said, "Francie, there ain't nothin' we can do about that poor boy but pray and hope for the best. I think he's long gone anyway. Now go to sleep. We got tomorrow's work plus gettin' ready for your daddy's homecomin'."

I let out a last shuddery sigh and kept my lips pressed together against all that I was feeling.

Serving on a Budget

At breakfast the next day Mama reminded me that we had the Grace tea to serve. I hadn't wanted to think about it. Mama would be needing me all day, to wax and polish and get the finger foods together.

I stopped in the middle of dishing up Prez's oatmeal. He opened his mouth to say he wanted more, but I was protesting before he could get the words out.

"Mama, I don't want to serve at Mrs. Grace's."

"Get a move on, Francie," Mama said, busy at the mirror getting her hat on, and not listening. "You gonna have to grab a couple of biscuits cause you ain't got time for oatmeal. We gotta go."

"Mama, I don't want to serve at . . ."

Mama looked over at me. "What?"

I thought about telling her why but decided against it. “Nothing, Mama.”

Holly Grace was nibbling on a cookie as she opened the back door. She looked me and Mama up and down, then turned and walked away. “Mother,” she called out, “the colored girls are here.”

I checked Mama to see what she thought about being called a girl, but she acted like she hadn’t even heard it. She pushed open the screen door and stepped into the kitchen. I followed her. I’d helped Mama at the Graces’ before and knew where things were kept. I started collecting what we’d need, while Mama went to get special instructions from Mrs. Grace. I could hear their voices in the dining room on the other side of the kitchen door.

Just then, Holly Grace came through the door and stood staring at me coldly. I pretended not to notice.

“Don’t you be spreading lies about me.”

I said nothing.

“Cause if you do—I’ma make sure you get in *big* trouble.”

I didn’t know how she’d do it, but I figured she had something in mind.

“You listening to me?” She tossed her hair. I measured the flour into a mixing bowl for monkey bread.

When Holly Grace reached the door, she gave me a look meant to seal her words on my mind, I was sure. I just went on with my work. But I was thinking: *thief, thief, thief.*

"Now, Lil," Mrs. Grace was saying to Mama over the platter of shrimp wheels me and Mama had just finished making. "I'm counting on you to make sure no one gets more than two of these shrimp wheels."

A whoop of laughter sounded from outside. Holly and her friends were sitting at the outdoor table under the big live oak playing cards. "Now, once you've determined a guest has had her two, Francie, you only go over to them with the tuna fingers." Mrs. Grace checked my face closely. "You understand that, Francie?"

"Yes'm." Mama frowned at me. "Yes, ma'am," I corrected myself. Mama didn't like me to sound slack around grownups.

Mrs. Grace sighed, patted her hair, and swished out.

"You need to take these out to them girls." Mama handed me a tray of glasses of iced tea. She noted my pout. "Go on, now. This is heavy."

Slowly, I took the tray from her. Mama stepped in front of me and held the door open. I made my way carefully down the back steps and the sloping lawn to where the girls sat fanning themselves and concentrating on their cards.

I placed a glass beside each of the four girls. Only one, Eva May Holland, murmured, "Thank you."

As I turned to go, Holly said, "Wait a minute. This needs more sugar." She held the glass out to me.

She was shielding her eyes at me and cocking her head. I took the glass, then made my way back up the slope to the kitchen. I put a teaspoon of sugar in her glass, stirred it, and tasted it. It tasted fine, but I dumped another teaspoon in it just in case.

Then I took it back to Holly, deposited it into her waiting hand, and started back to the kitchen. "Hold on, now," she called after me.

I looked back and caught her slyly smirking at one of her friends. "Not enough sugar still."

"Pardon me?"

"It's not sweet enough. Take it back."

"Did you give it a stir?" I'd put spoons and napkins on the table with the iced tea.

"What's that got to do with the price of rice in China?"

Betty Jo Parnell burst into giggles at this. I glanced over at her fat, sweating face.

"Well, the sugar has probably sunk to the bottom. If you stir every once in a while—"

"If you'd just put enough sugar in it in the first place, I wouldn't have to worry myself with stirrin' it all the time." Holly Grace held it out to me. I took it and went up the sloping lawn again. Once in the kitchen, I counted to twenty, then took it right back out to her.

She took a sip, smacked her lips, and announced, "Now, that's better." Then, with a whisk of the back of her hand, she waved me away.

I went back up the hill, grinning.

Mama put a tray of shrimp wheels in my hands as soon as I came into the kitchen, and directed me toward the dining-room door. “Remember, no more than two per customer. They pretty big, so ain’t nobody gonna be able to take more than two. Most’ll take just one, so you have to remember who took two and who took one when it’s time to go around again.” Mama opened the door for me and nodded her head toward the waiting guests. The tray was heavy, but Mama was needed in the kitchen to get the tuna fingers ready to go.

I advanced toward Mrs. Montgomery first—a familiar face.

“Thank you, Francie,” she said, plucking a shrimp wheel off the tray, then resting it on a napkin on her palm.

I went to Betty Jo Parnell’s mama next. She was deep in conversation, with her back to me. There wasn’t room to get around her. Besides, the lady she was talking to, Miss Rivers, was bound to notice me. Then I could offer them both the tray.

“He knocked him out stone-cold, don’t you know,” Mrs. Parnell said.

“I hope they catch that boy soon.”

“Oh, they will, I’m sure. My Henry is on it and they’ve enlisted some men up in Benson, too.” She took a sip of punch. “Oh, he’ll be caught. It’s just a matter of when.”

Miss Rivers noticed me then and gave Mrs. Parnell a little warning nod. She whirled around, all bright smiles, and said, "Well, don't mind if I do." She took a napkin and two shrimp wheels, stacking one on top of the other.

"I'ma need your mama a week from Saturday, Francie," Miss Rivers said. "Please tell her."

"Yes, ma'am." I made my way to the next cluster of white ladies, with my ears tuned to talk of Jesse. By the time I got back to the kitchen with the empty tray, there was a pain in my heart. Mama had a sandwich ready for me and I ate it standing at the kitchen counter, though with every bite I kept thinking: through the door are the wives of men who might think nothing of killing Jesse if they so decided. I was serving them finger food and grinning and being polite. I hated this. I wished I was on my train, leaving this place forever.

Mrs. Grace poked her head in the door just then to tell me to take a tray of shrimp wheels down to Holly and her guests.

With the heavy tray, I made my way down the slope. Betty Jo Parnell, her plump body squeezed into her shirred-bodiced sundress, took a slow sip of her tea. Selma Sutter, the richest of the group—her father owned Sutter Pulp Mill down near the river and half the land of the county, it seemed—had her brow furrowed over her cards. Eva May Holland, the beauty of the group, was watching Selma closely, her lips holding back a tiny smile.

A plan formed in my mind and with every step it took shape. With every step I grew excited by its perfection. It would work, God willing, if I did it just right. Did it in such a way that I could not be blamed. All I had to do was act stupid—act just the way they expected.

"Oh—Mama's shrimp wheels," said Holly Grace when I reached them. "Listen, you all, these are an absolute delight. Wait until you taste them."

"Two for each," I said, all sweetness and light.

Holly gave a little snort, looked over at Selma like I was some ninny, and said, "We'll certainly have as many as we like." She placed first one on her napkin, then another, then started to reach for a third. But I moved the tray to the side before she could do it. She looked up, her eyes blinking with astonishment. "What do you think you're doing?"

She had swam right to my bait and clamped down hard. "I'm doing what your mama told me to do and I gotta take my instructions from her." I started serving the other girls, which infuriated Holly.

"What in the world are you talking about?" She glanced first at Eva May Holland, then at Selma Sutter. Fat Betty Jo she didn't worry about. "We can have as many as we darn well please."

"I don't want to get in no trouble. I'ma have to tell your mama that you wouldn't listen that you all was to get only two each."

"That's ridiculous—you idiot—you must be making that up."

"No, ma'am. Your mama is serving on a budget and she said to make sure that nobody at this tea gets more than two shrimp wheels. She just can't afford it since your daddy messed up a lot of his money on a bad investment." I stopped short. I was saying too much and it might make her suspicious. She started to rise out of her chair. I backed up a little.

Holly caught her breath and a blush began from her neck to the top of her head until everything rising out of her bodice was bright crimson. Her lips moved but nothing came out. She checked her guests. They stared back. Betty Jo slowly set her own shrimp wheel down, looking slightly mortified.

"For Pete's sake, Betty Jo, you're not believing such foolishness, are you?" She shot a look to Selma, then to Eva May, who were also putting their shrimp wheels on their napkins and pushing them away. "I can't believe you all would pay any kind of attention to this simpleton."

Selma stared at her hands. Eva May looked off toward the house. An embarrassed silence filled the air. Finally Betty Jo, who wasn't as bright as the others and therefore too straightforward, said in a whining voice, "Well, Holly, let's face it—everybody knows your daddy did have that spell of financial—*bad luck*, so—"

"Shut your mouth, Betty Jo. That just ain't so."

"Actually, Holly," Eva May piped up, "I really think I'm allergic to seafood anyway. The last time I had lobster, I broke out in hives." Holly whipped around in her direction and just stared. Her eyes narrowed with disdain.

"You stupid idiot," she said, her attention back on me.

"Take them things back up to the house. We don't want any." Holly Grace sat down. When I hadn't moved, she blew up. "Take 'em!" she said. I returned each to the tray, noting all the while how each girl seemed embarrassed and uneasy. Holly picked up her cards and took a sip of tea, in an attempt to put the whole thing right out of her mind.

But as I made my way back up the hill to the kitchen, I knew she wouldn't be able to. Like I was gonna remember that slap, she'd remember this—always.

Waiting on Daddy

"What you doin'?" Prez asked, coming up behind where I sat on the porch steps in the twilight, staring at the woods. Juniper was darting in and out of the edge, chasing some poor creature for fun. Mama had washed my hair in castile soap. We all had our baths in the big tin tub in the kitchen. Now I sat on the steps, letting my hair dry in the last of the sun's heat. As it dried, it slowly grew into a woolly bush around my face. Mama was going to straighten it after she finished baking Daddy a welcome-home cake. Prez soon brought out a bowl and was licking a wooden spoon full of chocolate icing.

"Here," he said. "You get half."

I picked up the other spoon and licked some of the chocolate off. Prez drew a line with his finger down the center of the bowl. "This my side and this yours," he said, pointing to the two halves. I ran my finger along my side and came up with a nice helping of chocolate frosting.

"Whatcha doin' out here?" Prez asked.

"Watching the woods."

Prez had on his overalls and no shirt, his arms all coppery from the sun. He was what people called rhiny, with sandy hair bleached lighter at the temples. He had the same hazel eyes as Daddy's mama, who died when I was ten and Prez was seven.

"What for?" he said.

"Because Jesse Pruitt's in our woods."

"How you know that?"

"I feel it."

"Then they'll come down here and get him," he said, running his finger around the top of his side of the bowl, stopping exactly at the line he'd drawn.

"Right. And we gonna get some food to him and some money so he can get on. We gonna help him get away."

Later on, Mama took out the hot comb and heated it on the stove. She sat me in the kitchen chair.

"Bend your head and hold your ear," she said when she thought the comb had heated enough. I held my ear and my breath at the same time. When the heavy iron comb was that close to my face, I was afraid to breathe. It sizzled as Mama slid it through a place where the hair was still damp. "This part ain't dry enough," she said.

I stayed quiet. I wasn't going to chance a word. I'd been burned on the ear too many times from making an unexpected move. "Bend your head way down," she said. "Touch your chin to your chest."

I arched my head down as far as I could and felt the heat close in on the nape of my neck. The *kitchen*, Mama called it. The hardest part to straighten. Each time the heat moved away—the comb being placed on the fire again—I exhaled deeply and relaxed until Mama reached for it again to hold against the cloth to see if it was too hot, hot enough to leave brown teeth marks on the cloth. Then she waved it slowly through the air to cool it, her eyes far-off and patient. Thinking of Daddy coming tomorrow, I bet.

That night, in bed, I smelled vanilla. Mama must have put a couple of dabs behind her ears.

The morning was full of anticipation. While Mama pumped the water for boiling feathers off the chicken, she squinted up the road. As she stoked the fire in the stove, a noise outside made her move quickly to the porch to look out. She sewed a new patch on Prez's pants, and her eyes were constantly moving to the open door to look down Three Notch Road. Each time she turned from the door, or the window, or stepped back into the house, a flash of disturbance showed on her face that I didn't like.

I watched her closely and carried the weight of Mama's waiting as well as my own. Soon I couldn't stand it any longer. I had to get out. I'd go and pick flowers for the Sunday pitcher. Mama used it as a vase because it had a chip on its lip. "Get the watermelon out the creek," Mama called after me as I skipped down the steps. She had me put one in there the day before, so it could get cool.

Prez came along and we walked in silence. Then he piped up with, "What you think Daddy is gonna bring us from the road?"

"I don't know." I was busy wondering if maybe we should take this opportunity to search around for Jesse.

"You think some of them red swizzle sticks with the little monkeys on them?"

"I said I didn't know." He was quiet then, sulking. "Maybe some of them little soaps shaped like seashells like he brought us once," I said to make him feel better.

"I don't want no soap."

We closed in on the place where wildflowers grew in abundance. We picked black-eyed Susans and coneflowers and some goldenrod. Just as I was leading the way into the woods for some nice fern, Perry called out to us from the road. He had his fishing pole and a bucket of bait. Without even a word to me, Prez laid his flowers at his feet and started to trot off toward Perry.

"You better ask Mama about going fishing," I called after him. I was angry that he was running off and deserting me.

"Mama won't care."

"Ask her, then."

He was only a few minutes in the house. Then he was out again, running up the road with Perry, laughing and waving back at me. I could have slapped him. The only reason Mama was letting him go, I knew, was because she was wound up and she wouldn't have the quiet of mind she needed, having Prez underfoot asking when was Daddy coming.

Dry grass whipped at my ankles as I climbed down a small slope that led to some flowers I wanted that grew at the bottom. I forgot what they were called, but I loved how each green thistle shot out its furl of lavender like a bright promise.

The sun's rays warmed me and made me thirsty. My hair was still rolled in the rags from the night before. Now it was getting all sweated out. If I didn't get out of the sun, it wasn't going to be pretty as I'd planned for when Daddy got home. I looked at the stand of pine ahead. I'd go on and get that watermelon, and some fern, too, while I was at it.

Carefully, I laid my bouquet down and entered the woods, following the footpath that led to the creek. Soft pine needles felt good to my bare feet, as did the cool damp clay beneath that. I could hear Prez and Perry in the distance on their way to the pond. Light filtered through the changing pattern of leaves above, and an odd smoky scent in the air grew stronger as I neared the creek.

Someone had made a cooking fire, I thought. I slowed and stopped, scouring the dense growth around and ahead. I listened for some shift in the air, then continued toward the creek.

I ran into Prez and Perry sidetracked by the creek and all it had to offer. With pant legs rolled up, they shared the flattened top of a boulder. Prez was skipping pebbles over the water's surface. Perry was hunched forward, watching. They looked over at me.

"We came to get the watermelon, but someone ate it," Perry said.

"A hobo got it," Prez said stupidly.

"Or was it you two?" I asked.

"You just put it in the creek yesterday. How we have time to eat a whole watermelon?"

"What you think happened to it, Francie?" Perry whined.

I didn't bother to answer. I looked around. Everything seemed right. But there on the ground, hidden under the cover of damp leaves, were shiny black watermelon seeds and several wedges of rind. "Jesse Pruitt was here."

"Where!" both boys said at once.

I took a deep breath. "I smell his fire."

They followed suit, expanding their chests. Prez squinted. "I do smell it, too."

"And he didn't hit no Bellamy," I said.

"How you know?" Perry asked.

"Jesse wouldn't be that stupid."

"He supposedly knocked him out," Prez said, skipping a pebble.

"I don't believe it."

"I think they gonna get Jesse," Perry said.

"Shut up, fool," I said. He was making me mad.

"I'ma tell you said 'fool,' " Prez threatened.

"Tell. I don't care." I pretended to be looking up at the branches overhead. But I held my head back to keep the tears at bay. "Anyway, I think Jesse will get to the Southern Pacific and it will take him all the way to California.

"We'll take care of him until he can get away. I'll give him the money I got saved, and we'll bring him food." Both boys looked at me with admiration, which made me feel clever.

It was time to get back. Daddy might be there already and wondering where we were. I had to get the flowers in the Sunday pitcher and the rags out of my hair. I had to tell Mama that we didn't have no watermelon. "You all still going fishing?"

"Yea," Perry said quickly.

"Naw," Prez said, shaking his head. "I want to see if Daddy's come."

As soon as we stepped out of the woods and I looked across the open field to our house, I knew it held disappointment. Perry and Prez ran ahead. I hung back and slowly made my way over to where I'd laid down my bouquet. Mama would probably be on the porch by now, driven there by a waiting that no longer could be contained inside the house. She'd be shelling peas or shucking corn, but her eyes would be mostly on the road. And her thoughts would be full of preparing for disappointment. We'd been disappointed enough times before, so that by now I always held back some of my happiness at good news, and I knew Mama did, too.

Course she'd be preparing for him, too. Just in case.

It was early afternoon. There had been no set time for Daddy to arrive. Last summer, after he'd been gone for three months, he just showed up late one night. I'd woken up, hearing his voice coming from the kitchen. As soon as I was sure it was not part of a dream, I'd gotten out of bed and found him sitting at our table across from Mama, sipping a steaming cup of coffee. How wonderful my daddy looked. How wonderful it had been to crawl into his lap, to breathe his smell of tobacco, Old Spice, and sweat.

I had been glad that Prez, sound sleeper that he is, was still snoring away, unaware of anything but some silly dream he was probably having, and for a few minutes, while Mama had busied herself making Daddy a late supper and before she could think to shoo me back to bed, I had had Daddy all to myself.

Mama wasn't on the porch. She wasn't in the house. Maybe she was down to Auntie's, trying to get her mind off the waiting. Auntie was feeling stronger, we were happy to know. Daddy's homecoming cake sat in the middle of the kitchen table and the stove was crowded with good food. Corn bread and fried chicken, greens and corn on the cob. I was suddenly hungry. We seldom got such good food all at once.

I went over to the pantry, opened the door, and checked the jars of fruits and vegetables. I put a couple of jars of turnips into our croker sack, and a jar of beets. I snuck a jar of Mama's special pickled peaches and said a little prayer that she wouldn't notice.

"Take this and hide it by the outhouse," I said to Prez, handing him the sack. "We'll take it in the woods as soon as we can."

"I Gotta Help Him"

Mama didn't get back from Auntie's until just before dinnertime. Her face was as readable as a stone. She walked over to the pantry and got out a jar of pickled peaches and set it on the table.

"Wash up for dinner," she said. I let out the breath I'd been holding when Mama went into the pantry.

We ate in silence—neither Prez nor me having the nerve to ask any questions. We only spoke to ask that things be passed. I snuck a look at the cake now on the pantry counter, wanting some but afraid to ask. Besides, just because Daddy hadn't showed yet didn't mean that he wasn't going to show at all.

. . .

I awakened the next morning in a warm glow of expectation that lasted for a few seconds, until I remembered. Daddy had not come in the night. I felt his absence even before I slid out of bed for my trip to the outhouse. I met Prez on the way back. "Daddy didn't come," he said, his mouth sagging with disappointment. It always took Prez a while for things to sink in.

"No—he ain't coming, I guess."

"I should've gone fishing."

I had nothing to say to that.

I got dressed, put a couple of cold biscuits in my pocket, splashed some water on my face, and walked down to Auntie's. I climbed the steps to her door and heard Miss Mabel's voice coming from inside.

"Let me tell you, Lil and Lydia, I ain't never been so scared in my life."

I stood on the porch and listened.

"I was in the woods goin' after my headache leaf and I heard this noise that weren't no animal noise. Liked to scare me to death. I looked where that noise come from and there was that colored boy all hunched down in the bushes."

"What you do, Mabel?" Mama asked.

"I got outta there as fast as I could. That's what I did."

I peeked through the door.

"It won't be long before they come this way looking for him and it be best if we didn't give them folks no cause to get mad at us people on Three Notch," Miss Mabel said. I turned and tiptoed down the steps. I was going to the woods. I was going to find Jesse.

It was quiet. I got the jars Prez had hidden by the outhouse and set them beside the creek, then sat on the boulder, listening. I aimed my face at the shaft of light cutting through the network of branches overhead and saw it alive with tiny white flies. Jesse was close. I could feel it.

I wanted to call out his name, but I didn't know who else might be nearby. I threw my head back and closed my eyes. This was fine for now. I'd brought food. That'd be a help to him. I'd bring money as well. And maybe I could ask Miss Lafayette for advice. I slipped off the boulder and sloshed back to the creek bank, squatting to conceal the jars in the brush, but not too hidden that Jesse wouldn't see them.

There was a rustle nearby, but all I saw was a rabbit making a break for it.

Tuesday, Miss Beach and Treasure watched me and Mama come up the hill. Not our usual day, but Miss Beach needed us. She picked up Treasure from her lap, set him aside, and went into the house. She met us in the kitchen with her list of special instructions. One boarder wanted special attention paid to his collars and cuffs; another wanted light starch in his shirts, another wanted heavy. I watched Mama record these requests in her head and wondered how she could remember them all.

As soon as Miss Beach finished with my instructions—I was to polish the parlor furniture that day as well—I slipped upstairs. Just as I was about to knock on Miss Lafayette's door, she opened it. Her face registered surprise.

"Francie," she said, putting her hand to her chest. "I didn't even know you were coming today. How's Lydia doing and that fine baby girl I heard she had?"

"She's better now."

"Good, Francie."

"My daddy was supposed to come Sunday, but he didn't show," I blurted out.

Miss Lafayette frowned. "You must be disappointed."

"He's done that before."

"But still . . ."

"Miss Lafayette," I said, jumping ahead. "They're after Jesse."

"I know." She'd just gotten back into town, yet she'd already heard.

"They said he hit ol' Bellamy out at the Early farm."

She'd been standing. Now she sat down on the edge of the bed. "I don't believe it," she said.

"I don't believe a word of it either, Miss Lafayette. But they're after him and I think he's hiding out in our woods."

She sighed, thinking.

"I left him some food. By the creek."

"Francie." She pulled me down beside her and looked at me closely. "Listen to me. What you're doing is dangerous. Do you know what they'd do to your family if it was discovered you were aiding that boy in any way—what would happen to the colored community around here?"

"I gotta help him."

"You might not be able to."

"I have to." Tears filled my eyes. I grabbed her laundry bag and hurried out.

Mama and I got the linen and things washed, wrung out, and hung up by noon. Then I went to work on the parlor. When I got around to the old piano, I raised the lid carefully and placed my fingers on the keys. I wondered if Daddy was really gonna get me piano lessons. I wondered if I could count on him.

Signs in the Woods

I hadn't planned to go to the woods. My feet just guided me there. As soon as the idea took hold, I almost danced across Miss Beach's wide lawn to the road. I had to check my jars.

As I neared our house on Three Notch in the late afternoon, I saw Prez standing in the middle of the road, looking at me. I could sense his excitement.

"You got something to tell me?" I said right off.

He just looked at me with his eyes big and his mouth pressed together as if he had to clamp it shut on his news until he thought about how he'd say it. He jumped a little in place, then fell into step with me.

"You can't come with me," I said. I didn't want him tagging along.

"I been to the creek and I seen the jars." It seemed to spill out against his will. He looked surprised as soon as the words were said. "Me and Perry went to the woods after our time at the Earlys'."

"What are they saying over there?"

"Nothing to us." He kicked at a rock in the road.

"You seen Bellamy?"

"Yea, and I can't tell that anything happened to him. He's just fine and as mean as ever."

"What'd you see in the woods, Prez?"

"They empty!" He stopped walking and gave me a big loony grin.

"Come on."

First we had to stop by the house. I went straight for the pantry to get something new to take to the woods. Prez stood behind me, watching me make my decision.

"I'm gonna give him another jar of Mama's pickled peaches."

"You better not. Mama'll miss 'em."

"She got ten jars," I said, not really convinced that that would keep her from missing two. I rearranged what was left behind the jars of last year's summer squash and tomatoes. "She might not remember how many jars she had in the first place." I looked at Prez to see if he believed me. He looked as doubtful as I felt.

"Mama counts 'em," he said.

"She'll think she counted wrong."

Prez didn't say anything else. His lower lip quivered. He could be such a scaredy-cat.

"Prez, you wanna give him something to eat, don't you? Remember how pitiful he was? Big ol' boy and he couldn't even read . . ."

"Mama can't read."

"Mama's grownup. Lots a grown folks can't read," I said, trying to decide if I should take *Aesop's Fables* off the little shelf over my bed and leave it with the food. No, I decided. It would get messed up or carried off by animals or something.

"Come on. We need to get back before Mama gets home."

The woods in late afternoon had a mysterious dream-like light that made me hurry ahead.

"Wait up," Prez whined.

I slowed and let him catch up. He took my hand. I let him do that, too. We reached the creek and I knelt down and searched the brush until my hand felt the first cool glass jar. I lifted it up and saw it really was empty! A second one, too! Hmmph! I thought. I replaced the jars with the one I'd brought, carefully placing the empty ones in my sack. I looked over at Prez and couldn't help the big smile sliding over my face. "I knew it." I threw my head back. "Jesse's in our woods!"

Mama was sliding jars around in the pantry and muttering softly to herself. I could hear her counting behind my back as I sat at the kitchen table reading *The Dream Keeper.* Prez was quietly drawing—off in his own world. I nudged him under the table with my foot and he looked up, frowning at me, until he realized I was lifting my chin to draw his attention behind me. His eyes widened. I could feel him thinking: Uh-oh.

Mama's muttering grew louder. "One, two, three, four . . . five . . . I know I had ten jars of pickled peaches, ten jars of turnip greens, and I'm missing some black-eyed peas, for sure."

I felt Mama look over at me. I kept on reading.

"You two been in them peaches?"

I didn't say anything.

"Did you hear what I asked you?"

"We didn't eat any, Mama," I said truthfully.

"What happened to 'em, then?"

"We borrowed them."

Mama came around the table and gazed down at me, ignoring Prez. "And the turnips and greens?"

"It's for that boy they're after. I *know* that boy, Mama. He was in my class for a while last year." I closed the book over my finger and watched her closely, trying to read her face for what she was going to do to me. She sat down heavily, looking more perplexed than angry. She shook her head slowly.

"Mama, I know he's there and I know he's hungry."

"Francie, what am I going to do with you? What you're doing is dangerous, pure and simple. You can't be leaving food off in the woods for those white men runnin' around huntin' for him to find. They gonna look right to us cause those are our woods. We all gonna get in trouble, if they find that food. You get them jars out of there as soon as mornin' comes. You hear me?"

I didn't argue.

"You understand me, Francie?"

"Yes, ma'am." And I wasn't lying. I did understand Mama's point.

"We'll pray that boy's long on his way and it's just some hobo's been eatin' my food."

"What about what Miss Mabel said. That she seen him."

"Miss Mabel just wants attention. And she'll say anything to get it."

Mama got up then, took her sweater off the hook by the door, and slipped it on. There was the smell of rain in the air. Past her through the open door I could see dark clouds had gathered and now hung low. I shivered, thinking of Jesse out there in the woods.

"I'm going down to sit with Auntie. Give her some company. You remember what I said, Francie."

"Yes, ma'am." I'd remember it, but I wasn't going to heed it—not yet.

Sheriff Barnes

The next morning, I woke up to a long list of chores. Mama was already washed and dressed and twisting her hair into a knot. She jabbed it with a hairpin and it stayed. "I'm working for a friend of Mrs. Montgomery's today. You need to stop by Mrs. Grandy's and pick some of that headache leaf she got growin' by her house, for Auntie. Perry came down to tell me that she's feeling poorly again."

She walked over to me. "And needs her cow milked, too." She pushed at my shoulder, thinking I'd gone back to sleep.

"I'm awake, Mama."

"Auntie needs some things washed and ironed, and have Prez and Perry round up some kindling. She's runnin' low."

It seemed that Mama was going to go on and on forever. I was happy to see her walk out the door. "But you get them jars before you do anything," she said over her shoulder. I rolled my eyes, sitting there among the rumpled sheets. The sun was hardly up.

Mama had left some cold biscuits on the table and a saucer of maple syrup. I sat down, dropped a biscuit in my shift pocket, and ran the edge of another through the syrup. I nibbled on it as I padded barefoot down the hall to wake Prez. He was curled up, his bedclothes kicked onto the floor, his mouth gaping open, and his snore a light whistle. I gave him a hard shove. He muttered something and swatted at his face. I pushed him again.

"Stop that!"

"You gotta get up." I was feeling mean.

"Why?"

"Cause you gotta get over to Auntie's and milk her cow." I didn't say: *Mama said.* If he thought so—it wasn't my fault.

He pouted. "Why can't Perry do it?"

"You know he's been too scared to, since Millie kicked him."

"It ain't fair."

"Too bad." I pushed at his shoulder. "Get up!"

Perry was playing Jack in the dirt by the porch as we walked up. "Come on, Jack, get on the stick," he said, peering down in a hole.

"You got one?" Prez asked.

"Got more than one. And there's another one down there."

"Here, let me try," Prez said, reaching for the thin jonquil branch that Perry was carefully twirling in the hole.

"Naw—you gotta wait until I'm good and finished." He turned the stick. "There," he said, pulling it out slowly with a jack bug clinging to the end. Perry raked it into a mason jar to join two others. He twisted the top, then held it up so he could examine his bugs more closely.

Prez and I leaned in for a better look. "I'm next," Prez said. He spit on a clump of dirt and mixed it with the twig until it was the right thickness to stick to the end. Carefully he lowered it into the hole and began to turn it gently. We held our breath. Then something far off disturbed the quiet air.

A car was approaching. I shielded my eyes and squinted at the distant cloud of red dust.

"It's the sheriff," Perry said. We watched as the big, shiny black roadster turned down Three Notch and crept toward us. Two men in wide-brimmed hats sat in the front.

We stood up. I nudged Prez's elbow with my own as the sheriff got out of his car and made his way over to us. He looked back at his deputy, whose eyes seemed to be boring into the woods with suspicion.

"How y'all doin' today?" His eyes slid over the boys, then settled on me.

"We're fine, Sheriff," I said.

"Whatcha all doin'?"

"Playin' Jack," Prez offered before I could answer.

I shot him a sideways glance. I didn't want him to start running his mouth. He could be careless.

"How you do that?"

"We catch 'em on this here twig," Prez said, unaware of my signal.

Sheriff Barnes wasn't paying any attention, however. He was looking toward the house.

"Where's your mama?" he said to Perry.

Perry looked back. "In the house."

"What about your daddy. He over at the Early farm?"

"No, sir. He work over in Benson."

Now the deputy—Withers was his name—stepped out of the car and was wiping the back of his neck with a red handkerchief oily with dirt and sweat. He pulled a piece of paper out of his back pocket and unfolded it carefully. It was that same picture of Jesse that I saw posted behind the register at Green's.

"You seen this boy?" Jesse Pruitt's sorrowful face stared back at us. I stiffened and felt Prez and Perry stiffen, too. The deputy must have picked up on it. "Don't you lie, now." He squinted down at us.

I didn't have to lie. "We ain't seen him," I said.

The deputy looked over at Sheriff Barnes, then back to me. "You know who he is?" he asked.

"He was in my class in the spring for a few weeks."

"You know him, then," Sheriff Barnes said, perking up.

"Yes, sir. He was in my class."

"But you ain't seen him."

"No, sir."

He let a few seconds go by. "You sure?"

"Yes, sir. I'm sure I ain't seen him," I said firmly and shook my head.

Withers kept his eyes on me as he folded up the paper and tucked it into his back pocket. He turned and started for the house, leaving Sheriff Barnes rubbing his chin and looking around.

As he passed Prez and Perry, he chucked them on the back of the head, playfully but hard—both boys winced from the pain.

Withers had to pound on the door for what seemed like a long time. Finally, Auntie cracked the door, holding her robe up at her neck. She leaned on the doorjamb. They showed her Jesse's picture. She took the paper out of the deputy's hand and held it in her trembling hand. She shook her head slowly from side to side, then handed the paper back. Sheriff Barnes, now on the porch, said something to her while Withers folded his precious paper, turned his head toward the steps, hocked, and spit.

They didn't drive toward town when they left. They made their way slowly up Three Notch and for some reason passed Miss Mabel's and stopped in front of our house. They banged on the door a few times, then tried the knob. Finding it unlocked, they went in.

"They going in our house," Prez said.

"I can see," I said.

Before long, Sheriff Barnes came out with a hunk of Daddy's cake in his hand, his mouth so full it was pushing out both cheeks.

"He's eatin' Daddy's cake," Prez said.

I went over to the deputy's glob of spit and kicked dirt over it.

They circled back to Miss Mabel's next. "She's gonna tell 'em something," I said. I could feel it.

"Maybe not," Prez said hopefully.

I snorted at this. "I should have listened to Mama and got those jars out first thing. But I wanted to give Jesse a chance to discover them." I kicked at the dirt. "I'm going as soon as they leave. Prez, you go milk Millie. Perry, go on down to Mrs. Grandy's and get your mama some headache leaf. Stay out of the woods and let me take care of things."

Miss Mabel was now on her porch. All three figures leaned over the railing, focusing on the woods. "I knew it," I said.

"You think they gonna get the bloodhounds?" Perry asked.

I looked over at him, not liking him much right then. "Just go do what I said." The sheriff drove off toward the Grandys'. After a short while, the men were back in their car, driving in the direction of the woods. We stood openmouthed as they stopped their car, got out, and began walking. Soon the woods swallowed them up.

"Francie," Prez whimpered. "We gon' get it."

"Would you stop it? I gotta think."

"We gon' get in trouble. We gon' get the whole road in trouble," he insisted.

"Go do your work," I said.

I thought about Mama's jars, jars with Mama's labels on them. The ones I'd carefully written, myself: *From Lil's Kitchen.* I'd seen similar labels on Mrs. Montgomery's canned goods. "They're not going to find them," I said.

"How you know, Francie?"

"I got a feeling."

I did have a feeling. But that didn't keep me from looking for Sheriff Barnes and Withers to come out of the woods as I went about doing my work. It didn't keep my heart from sinking a little every time I looked up and saw that big black car still parked there.

Finally, just as I was setting up the washboard and tub to wash diapers, I spotted them getting into their car and driving off, empty-handed and alone.

With my heart in my mouth, I left the washboard in the tub, dried my hands, then went down the splintered steps and across the hot, dusty yard. I hurried along, but it didn't feel nearly fast enough.

The Bascombs

Once I was on the path to the creek, my fear grew. I decided to try a shortcut, pushing through brush and leaping over tree roots, until I heard something that stopped me as still as a frightened deer. Men's voices. Up ahead. Carefully, I made my way through the undergrowth.

White men. Two of them. I pictured Mama's mason jars lined up neatly by the creek, all nicely labeled. My breath came fast and shallow as I suffered through the thunderous sound of every rustling leaf.

Maybe I had imagined it. I waited, then continued, stepping even more cautiously. Those voices again. Not the sheriff and his deputy; other voices, steadily getting closer. With terror taking hold, I looked for a place to hide, all the time pushing down the urge to cry.

In back of me was brush dense enough to hide in. I ducked behind it and hunched down, struggling to hear what the voices were saying. To my horror, I heard Prez's voice—whimpering. Pleading. Then Perry's pleading in the same tone. I knew then what it meant to feel as if all your blood had drained away. I felt faint.

Gently, I parted small branches until I could see. Four figures came into view and I clamped my mouth with my hand. A small animal, perhaps, rustled the bushes and Billy Bascomb, gripping Prez by the arm, nearly lifted him off the ground, jerking his head around. Billy's eyes narrowed and bored into bushes near me. He slowly raised a palm.

"Wait . . ." he said, and Jack Bascomb, his arm wrapped around Perry's head, forcing him along that way, stopped.

"Thought I heard something."

"A rabbit . . ." Jack said. Billy searched in my direction—too high, thank God—but the moment hung there until he turned away.

I'd seen those two over the years. Billy's wife, Mary Jo, sometimes came by the Montgomerys' for a handout. Everybody knew Billy didn't hardly work if he could help it. They'd gotten to our woods and come upon Prez and Perry. I felt a stab of anger. I *told* those boys to stay out of the woods, and now their hardheadedness had gotten them square in this situation.

"Mister, honest—I didn't do nothing," Prez wailed.

"You comin' with us anyway. Now stop that blubbering. We takin' you to jail for aidin' and abettin'."

"We didn't do nothin'," Perry cried, sounding as if he was lying.

"Shut your mouth," Billy said through gritted teeth. "You was up to somethin' and we all know it."

For a frantic moment, I nearly rushed out from my hiding place, but fear paralyzed me. With repugnance, I saw Perry's whole shirtsleeve had been nearly ripped off. There was a bloody gash on his arm. I buried my face in my hands and squeezed my eyes tight, willing myself not to make a peep until their sounds faded away completely. *Perry was hurt.* I stood up, my legs nearly buckled, but I knew I had to get home.

I ran to the clearing and the bright afternoon light. There was Auntie's house. No cars, no sign of anything amiss. I looked down toward Mama's. Nothing to see but our small house vacant and alone.

"That you, Francie?"

"Yes, Auntie."

"Where you been?" She was struggling toward me, holding on to the wall. "Perry ain't come back yet with that headache leaf. Can you go down to Nola's and get me—"

"Auntie, they got Perry and Prez!" I blurted out before I could think about fixing up the words a little first.

"What?" Auntie continued toward me.

"Here, Auntie." I took hold of her and tried to direct her back to bed, but she pulled away and pushed past. She almost fell into the kitchen chair, then sat for a moment, catching her breath.

I paced a little, not wanting to tell her.

"Francie, what you sayin'? Out with it."

"I was in the woods . . ."

"What for?"

"I had to do something—real important."

Auntie just stared at me, perplexed.

"They were coming at me. And I had to hide behind some bushes . . ."

"Who? What are you talking about?"

"I seen the Bascomb brothers taking Perry and Prez out of the woods."

"Why would they be taking them *anywhere*?" Her face was full of confusion.

I hesitated.

"Francie, you tell me, now!" Janie woke up and began to cry from the bedroom. Auntie ignored her.

"We left some food for Jesse Pruitt. It was my idea, Auntie," I said quickly. "I had to wait until the sheriff come out of the woods and drove away before I could get the jars back—that's what I'd been leaving—some of Mama's canned goods. They'd see them with Mama's labels on them and we'd get in trouble." My words were coming out in a rush. "Perry and Prez were just supposed to do their work. I told them to stay out of the woods."

"Francie, I'm confused. What is it you're sayin' to me?"

I sat down. "They got the boys because they think they were helping Jesse. The Bascomb brothers."

Auntie's eyes grew big with horror. "They got those babies? Where they takin' them?"

"I don't know, Auntie," I lied.

Auntie ran her hands through her hair and searched the tabletop. "Where they takin' 'em!" she said, her voice rising with hysteria. Janie began to cry louder. Auntie's face drained of color. "Francie, you get them into this?"

I nodded weakly.

"You did somethin' that foolhardy?"

I nodded again.

"Where your brains, girl? Why not give them men an invitation to get mad at all the coloreds and burn us out just to make their point? Why not just put up a sign?"

I began to cry.

"Oh, my God . . . Where would they be takin' 'em?" she whispered into the air, as if that was all she could manage.

I looked away for a second. It was hard to bear the expression on her face. "They taking them to jail, Auntie," I finally admitted.

"To jail? Them two little boys? Was they hurt?" She asked this like she was afraid of the answer.

I thought of Perry's torn sleeve and his hurt arm, but I couldn't bring myself to relate this situation to Auntie.

"No'm," I said, feeling worse for it.

She slumped down in the chair and put her face in her hands. "How on earth am I going to get through this?"

I was crying in earnest now. I cried for myself because this was my fault, I cried for Perry and Prez and what they must be feeling, and for Mama, who was gonna be real scared and mad—when she found out.

Mama looked at me as if she hadn't heard. I'd been pacing the room for the last hour and looking out the window up the road for the first sign of her. Auntie had all that time sat immobile at the table, her face in her hands.

Mama now put her hand over her mouth, as if preventing herself from screaming out.

"We gotta do something. We gotta do something quick. Come on." She had taken off her town hat and set it on the table. And now, for some reason, she plucked it back up, plunked it on her head, and started for the door. Auntie went and picked up the now sleeping Janie and I followed her outside. But Mama stopped short at the bottom of the porch steps and said, "I don't know what we can do."

"Mama," I offered, "maybe Mr. Grandy can help us." Folks were always looking to Mr. Grandy for help. He was smart, he had his own land, and he was there with his family rather than off working the railroad or up in Benson working away from his family. And he seemed to always know what was happening behind the scenes.

Without a word, we made our way up the road toward the Grandys'.

I could tell by his face when he opened the door that Mr. Grandy didn't know what to think. We stood huddled there, crying on his front porch.

"Lil . . . Lydia? What's *wrong*?" Janie began to whimper as if on cue.

Mama spoke first. "O.C., Francie done a stupid thing and now they got our boys."

This didn't give Mr. Grandy any real information, but he motioned us inside. Mrs. Grandy and her daughter, Violet, who were sitting at the dinner table, stood up.

"Lil, what you talkin' about?" Mrs. Grandy said, coming forward and taking Mama by the shoulder. Violet helped Auntie into a chair, then Mama, for Mama seemed barely able to move at that point. She was stiff and her eyes were filled with fear. Violet went to get them both a drink of water. I started crying anew and Mama looked at me with disgust. The others took no notice of my personal misery. All were focused on Mama, and finally, too, Auntie with Janie in her arms.

"You tell us, now," Mr. Grandy said calmly. "You tell us what happened."

Mama took a deep breath and told them the story. When she finished, they turned their stunned faces to me. I looked down at my feet.

"Sheriff was out here this mornin'," Auntie added, "with a picture of that boy. Then Perry and Prez musta got it into their heads that they had to go get them jars of food out the woods before they were found—bringin' trouble on all us."

"I told them not to, Mama," I said, pleading my case. "I was going to take care of that myself. I knew I could do it without getting caught. But they didn't listen."

"That ain't the point, Francie!" Mama said, losing her temper, and I knew if we weren't at the Grandys' and Mama wasn't so scared, I would have gotten a back hand across the face for sure.

"So the sheriff caught 'em?" Mr. Grandy asked, putting Mama's tirade at me on hold.

"No," Mama said. "The Bascomb brothers were in the woods, probably hopin' they'd get a jump on them others the sheriff was roundin' up. They goin' after that reward money." Mama put her head down on her folded arms. "I pray they don't hurt our boys."

Auntie, who'd been looking back and forth between Mama and Mr. Grandy, watching how he was taking everything in, now said, "What can we do?"

Everyone turned to him then. Even Mrs. Grandy and Violet. He seemed to be searching for an answer, while a grave silence filled the room. We waited. Mama's eyes swept desperately back and forth between Mr. and Mrs. Grandy.

At once, the rumble of what sounded like a hundred cars began to approach from the distance. Mr. Grandy went quickly to the window and looked out.

"Kill that light," he said.

Violet leaned over the kerosene lamp and blew. The room instantly slipped into blackness.

Headlights played on the far wall. Before Mama could stop me, I was at the window peering out at the procession moving along the edge of the woods. I flinched at the flurry of yelps and snarls from Mr. Early's dogs. He was proud of those hounds. They were used to tracking. "They *love* it," Prez had heard him bragging one time. "You see, nigras got a particular smell and they can find one and zero right in."

"Where's my baby?" Mama said behind me. She was looking over my head, talking more to herself than to me.

"What's happening out there ain't got nothin' to do with those boys," Mrs. Grandy reassured Mama.

"That's right," Mr. Grandy agreed. "Them boys are probably in jail right now, gettin' a good scare."

Mama didn't answer. Her mind seemed to be on something else. Suddenly I felt her tense up. "Come on," she said all at once. "We gotta get home."

Before I knew it, we were on the small back trail, rushing toward home, with the Grandys watching us from their back porch, knowing there was no changing Mama's mind.

"They could've found their way home, somehow," Mama told us. "Could've learned their lesson and now they're wonderin' where we are."

With every step, our hopes grew. Until we came upon

the dark house with not one sign of life. Still, we hurried up the steps with the hope that perhaps the trucks and dogs and loud, drunken men had scared the boys into darkness and quiet.

Mama called out Prez's name as she went through the door. Silence was the dismal answer.

"They ain't here," Aunt Lydia said. Janie stirred in her arms as if she was disappointed, too. Mama wasn't afraid of light. She lit the kerosene lamp on the table, illuminating the sad room.

"What happened here?" she asked, pointing to the half-eaten cake sitting on the counter.

"Wasn't none of us, Mama. The sheriff and his deputy come by today while we were down to Auntie's. They had a picture of Jesse to show us. They came down here and went right in our house—and just took what they pleased."

Mama listened without a word. Then she took the cake platter over to a bag by the sink and, with a knife, raked what remained into it. Every last crumb.

"I'll make another," she said, but it was an empty promise. It had taken us long enough to save for the ingredients for the one she'd just thrown out.

"Maybe they got away and are hiding in the woods," Auntie said.

Mama shook her head solemnly. "They wouldn't be in no woods at night. They're both scared of their own shadows."

Auntie started to stand then, just to do something, but

Mama gently pulled her back down. "Please don't get yourself worked up . . ."

Auntie rocked and cried softly. "What are we going to do?" she said over and over.

"We just gonna wait."

But our wait was disturbed by snarls and the stubborn yelps of Mr. Early's excited hounds. Voices shouted back and forth for the next hour.

That hour passed slowly and painfully. Several times I wanted to put my head down on the table. I didn't dare. I was scared I'd fall asleep. Mama paced. Auntie wept with fear. From time to time, we joined hands and prayed.

I must have slept at some point. The next thing I knew, there was the sound of tires driving slowly around the side of our house. Mama and Auntie were at the window just as I was lifting my head from the table.

"What on earth . . ." Mama was saying.

"What on earth . . ." Auntie repeated. I squeezed in between them and looked out.

A shadowy figure sat behind the steering wheel of a long black car parked in our backyard. Something about it seemed odd. I squinted at the car window. Who *was* that? The door opened and Clarissa Montgomery got out and started for the door. Before she could knock, Mama had opened it and stood waiting, dumbfounded.

"Clarissa," I said.

"I've got your brother and cousin in my uncle's car," she said simply.

Mama rushed past her to the car. I stood there, peering into the night.

"Where are they?" I asked.

"In the back, on the floor. When I saw the men and heard the dogs, I cut my lights and told them to get down." Clarissa looked over her shoulder.

Mama yanked open the door and pulled out of the back seat, first Prez, then Perry. Frightened and huddled, they stumbled up the steps. Auntie grabbed Perry and drew him to her.

"Mama, I'm okay," he said, slipping out of her grasp.

She grabbed him and hauled him into the house. Prez, between Mama and Perry, followed meekly. Mama settled them both at the table, then just stared down at them for seconds. She and Auntie took in their bedraggled condition. Perry's shirt was torn, with only a scrap of sleeve hanging from the shoulder. His bare arm was wrapped in a dish towel. Blood showed through.

"My God . . ." Auntie cried, gently touching his arm. "What happened to you?" Perry began to cry, his attention back on his sorry state.

Prez was almost as bad. His hair was matted with leaves and his clothes were caked with dirt. He started sobbing, as if in sympathy.

Finally, between hiccups, Perry managed to get out, "I cut it trying to get away from one of them Bascomb brothers."

"What happened?" Mama asked.

"They was trying to haul us off to jail."

I looked over at Clarissa, who was surveying our front room. The sink pump, the kerosene lamp, Mama's Diller's Drugs calendar . . . She sat down without being asked and listened to Prez's story as if she'd never heard it before. Auntie interrupted him. "Girl, how'd you drive your uncle's car out here?"

"Prez told me a back way," Clarissa said.

"No. I mean, your uncle let you drive his car?" Auntie asked.

"I waited until I knew he was asleep. Then I rolled it down the driveway." Mama and Auntie studied her. "I saw the boys in the gazebo earlier in the evening, trying to hide, but I had to wait until everyone was asleep before I could go down and see what was going on."

She stopped and let that sink in.

"What were you doing in the Montgomerys' backyard?" Mama asked Prez. Prez always got tongue-tied when frightened.

"We were hiding there."

"Prez—don't try my patience. I know you were hiding there. Why? How?"

"We were just trying to get the jars after the sheriff came out, so nobody'd get in trouble," Prez cried. "Those Bascomb boys were gonna take us to jail!"

I cut him off to try and salvage my good name. "And I told you to just do your work. You know I did."

He only glanced at me. He was more interested in getting his side over to Mama.

"We decided to hide them instead. We hid them good, too," he said to me in particular. "We dug a hole . . ."

"But they run across us," Perry added, "and they said we looked suspicious and stuff. Then they grabbed us. 'Cept I got away for a minute, but I fell and hurt my arm. I scraped it real bad—else Jack Bascomb wouldn'ta caught me." He looked over at Prez. "Billy Bascomb already caught Prez." He took a breath.

"Only cause I fell, too," Prez said.

Auntie, standing behind Perry, had been rubbing his shoulders. Now she leaned down and looked at him closely.

"They threw us in their car, Mama. They said they were taking us to jail for"—he hesitated—"aidin' and abettin' a fugitive."

"They said all that, huh." Mama was getting angry.

"We got away when they stopped at the filling station."

"I think they let us get away," Perry cut in.

"Did not!" Prez insisted.

"I saw 'em laughing at us when we ran."

"Then whyn't you just walk on back, then? Tell me that!" Prez demanded.

"Don't start arguing among yourselves now," Auntie said on her way out of the room to see about Janie, who'd awakened for her midnight feeding.

"We was over on Cypress and Prez said they was gonna come after us and put us in jail for sure."

"I didn't say no such thing."

"Tell the truth and shame the devil," Perry said.

"You was the one who was runnin'." Prez turned to Mama. "He was the one who started runnin' in those white folks' backyards—hidin' out and such."

"Wasn't—"

"Shut up, both of you," Mama said quietly. She sighed and got up, went into the other room, and came back with the brown bottle of peroxide and some strips of muslin. "Let me see that," she said to Perry.

He drew back.

Clarissa, who'd been sitting with her chin in her hand for some time, perked up.

"Naw, Auntie. It's gonna hurt."

"Boy, if you don't give me that arm—you are gonna be hurt for sure."

Perry submitted. He scrunched his face and squeezed his eyes shut in preparation for pain.

"Ow, ow, ow . . ."

"Shut up now, you big baby—you know I ain't hurtin' you." Quickly Mama washed the wound and wrapped it in clean muslin. She bit the end of the strip and ripped it down the middle. She tied the bandage closed.

Perry seemed to slump then. "I'm tired, Mama."

Mama turned to Clarissa. "I want to thank you for bringing our boys back to us. But you go on home. Your people've probably discovered you gone by now and are worried sick."

Clarissa got up slowly and, it seemed, reluctantly. She

moved to the door. Mama reached past her and opened it for her. “Be careful, now. I sure thank you,” she said again.

Clarissa gave her a little nod and slipped out.

“They’re packin’ up,” Mama said. She’d not left her post by the window since Clarissa left. Sure enough, we could hear the motors being revved up. I joined her and looked out. A train of headlights was snaking up the road, heading our way. A pickup filled with loud, whooping men gunned past. Something cracked against the side of the house and we heard it shatter. An empty beer bottle, I was sure. Mama and I ducked down and waited until the sound of every car and truck had died away.

Auntie had snuck home with Perry and Janie, and Prez lay sound asleep in his bed when Mama said, “Bet they didn’t get him.”

“How do you know?”

“I got a feelin’.”

When the night settled into its quiet, we crawled into bed and fell immediately to sleep.

Jesse

I let Prez sleep through the morning while I worked on some pillow slips Mama was having me do for Auntie. I peeked in on him just to make sure he was still there. Before Mama had left for an emergency situation at the Montgomerys'—they were having unexpected overnight guests—she had told me not to let Prez out of my sight. I was excused from helping her.

A storm seemed promised for late morning. I had swept the yard and then sat on the porch, finishing the slips Mama had made me rip out and start over. "Your stitches are long and lazy. You know better than to get in a hurry," she said. I sat on the porch and watched rain clouds gathering.

I thought about Juniper. We hadn't seen him in days,

but I wasn't worried. He often went on excursions in the woods, only to emerge days later, hungry and full of ticks. I was really going to miss him when we moved, however. We couldn't take him with us, so Perry'd be getting him.

As if he'd read my mind, I spied Juniper running along the edge of the woods and disappearing back into it. I sewed a line of tiny stitches, then stopped to admire my handiwork. Mama was not going to make me rip these out, I thought. When I checked to see if I could glimpse Juniper again, I saw a man walking slowly across the field toward our house. Not Juniper.

It was Jesse, moving as if his legs weighed a ton, but not caring that he was crossing the open field in broad daylight. Reminding me of the first time I laid eyes on him last spring at school.

He walked right to the steps and stared at me without a word. I stood up and held the door open for him and he went inside. I took a good look at him then. His hair was caked with leaves and twigs and clumps of mud. His shirt was in tatters and he'd either lost his shoes or didn't have any on when he first went into hiding.

"I thought you were gone for good. How'd you hide from them dogs?"

"I ran along the creek for a good mile or two and came out when I thought I'd gone on long enough. Then I hid out till this morning."

"Why'd you try to beat up a white man?" I asked.

He sunk down into our kitchen chair.

"Can I have some water?" he asked. "And a little somethin' to eat?"

I got him the water and some of the corn bread left over from the day before. He pushed the corn bread into his mouth with filthy hands. Then, while his mouth was still full, he began to gulp down the water, his eyes nearly closed. I watched the rising and falling of his Adam's apple. He wiped his mouth with the back of his hand. "I'd like some more—if you don't mind."

I brought him another glass.

"Got any shoes I can have?"

I looked down at his muddy feet. "My daddy has some old shoes about your size." I went into the other room. "He's a Pullman porter now," I called out as I dug around in the bottom of the wardrobe. "They gave him a full uniform and new shoes. He wouldn't wear these now." I returned to the front room and set them down by his feet. He slipped his dirty feet easily into them and tied them up. I felt full of accomplishment, looking at his feet in my daddy's shoes.

"Did you do that fool thing that they said you did?" I asked, taking my seat across from him.

"I didn't go after nobody." His eyes were filled with anger. "I ain't crazy."

"Bellamy going around saying you did."

"Cause he lied on me." Jesse drank from his glass. "To save face."

I waited.

"The man ain't never paid me honestly. He was short-changing me. Laughing at me behind my back. I suspected as much, but I didn't know it until I heard one of the white workers laughing about how stupid I was. That I couldn't cipher. When I asked Bellamy about it, real polite like, he got mad and called me uppity. Told me there was plenty men who'd be glad to get my job."

Without warning, tears welled up in Jesse's eyes. He wiped them away. "I didn't say nothin' more about it—just did my job. But he fired me."

Silence settled between us while I tried to understand this different version. "I just took what was mine. One night I snuck in the Early henhouse to get a chicken. I figured that was what he owed me—at least. Bellamy come in before I could get away. I only run past him, s'all. And he fell. I got away. He must have decided he was gonna get me back. I heard what he sayin'—I assaulted him. But I didn't touch that man."

He stared at his hands. "I got me a plan," he said. "It's just gonna take me a few days to put it into motion, but . . ."

The sound of a car pulling up in front of the house interrupted him. It seemed to come out of nowhere. Jesse put a hand on my arm. I moved away and went quickly to the window in time to see the sheriff, alone, getting out of his car.

I was outside before he got to the steps to the front door. He'd parked in my freshly swept yard. Leisurely, and with deliberate slowness, I thought, he came over to stand at the bottom step. He flicked a cigarette butt in Mama's flower bed.

"Where's your brother?"

"Prez's asleep, sir."

"Go get him."

I backed into the house and did what I was told. The kitchen was deserted; Jesse had disappeared. I couldn't even imagine where. Mama had all her boxes of quilting scraps under Prez's bed. The pantry was too small. The bed me and Mama slept in stood so high nothing could be hidden under there. I dared not try to find him.

"Get up, Prez," I said, shaking him. "The sheriff wants you."

He sat up at once and started whimpering. "Why's he want me?"

"He didn't tell me." I looked around the room. "Hurry up."

Prez threw on his clothes and wiped the sleep out of his eyes. We hurried down our small hallway and came upon the sheriff standing in our kitchen. I stopped short. I looked around. Prez slipped his hands in the back pockets of his overalls and cast his eyes to the floor.

The sheriff stared down at him. "What were you doin' in the woods yesterday?"

"We was just going after kindling for my auntie, Sheriff," Prez said in a muffled voice.

"Speak up when I talk to you," the sheriff bellowed.

Prez looked up with fear, but he did not look in the man's eyes. "That's the only reason we was there, sir."

"Jack Bascomb said he caught you in the woods up to something."

"No, sir."

"You callin' him a lie?"

"No, sir," Prez said quickly. "I'm just saying we was only going after kindling."

"By the creek."

"We got to playing, sir." Prez's voice caught, and I knew he was struggling to hold back the tears.

"You weren't in them woods to help that boy we're after?"

"No, sir! I don't know nothin' about no boy." He broke down over his lie then. The sheriff looked down on him like he was disgusted and yet found Prez funny at the same time. He glanced over at me. "I need me some water."

Quickly, I moved to the pump and filled the glass Jesse had used and handed it to him. He downed the water and handed the glass back. He looked at me with a puzzled expression, as if it had just occurred to him to wonder about my part in this.

Suddenly my eye caught Daddy's boots, through the open door down the hall, in the dark space between the hem of the wardrobe curtain and the floor. My heart thumped in my chest. I turned toward the window, thinking my expression would surely give me away.

And if that didn't, my pounding heart. I felt my face flush hot.

"What's wrong?" the sheriff asked.

"I just remembered I ain't seen my dog for a while and I was hoping he didn't get torn up by one of those hounds last night."

The sheriff angled his head back and looked at me for a long time. Finally, he moved to the door. "I better not learn you two been up to something. You'll be sorry if I do." He shook his finger at us. A thick slab of a finger. "Don't let me find out you was lyin'."

As soon as he was gone, I brought my finger to my mouth and pointed down the hallway. Prez followed my pointing finger and his eyes grew big. He ran to the window and watched until the sheriff's car pulled away. "He's going down to Auntie's to talk to Perry."

Jesse stepped out of the wardrobe and wiped his sweating face. "I'ma go."

Prez's mouth dropped open. "We gonna get in trouble, Francie!" he cried.

"No, we ain't," I said. I turned to Jesse. "Where you going?"

He drew up, like he was trying to fill himself with confidence. "I'm gettin' down to New Orleans. I can catch a freight out to California from there."

For a second I envied him and wished I could hop a freight to California myself. Where the sun always shined and oranges grew on trees and the ocean was in your backyard. "Where you going to be until then?"

"Where I been."

"It ain't safe."

I took his hand and led him to the window. I pointed over to Miss Mabel's house. "You see that house down there? The woman who lives there saw you in the woods, and I know she told the sheriff and his deputy. I know it."

"She ain't gonna see me."

"Yes, she will. Because she's in the woods all the time, going after her plants. She'll know you're there. And if she thinks she can get something out of it, she'll tell."

He seemed to think about this.

"You can hide out in our shed."

"Uh-uh, Francie," Prez said. "We'll get in trouble."

I ignored him and just waited for Jesse's response.

"Okay," he said. He had no choice.

"The sheriff's gonna find out and he's gonna arrest us!" Prez whined.

"Be quiet, Prez. You don't know what you're talking about." I was moving around the room, gathering up what I thought he'd need. A blanket, some biscuits, a quart jar of water. I screwed the lid on tight and put everything in his arms. I got my own pillow off my bed and put it on top. Then I remembered the book Clarissa had given me for Jesse. I ran and got it.

"Here, take this, too. It's *Aesop's Fables.* The shed is out back. You can go get some sleep." We all looked out the window to see where the sheriff's car was. There was no sign of it. I opened the door and Jesse went through it, crossed my yard, and disappeared into the shed.

Then I watched that shed. While I rolled dough for biscuits and made hominy and gravy, I kept my eyes on it as much as possible. When Prez started for the door, I checked him. "Where you going?"

"Down to Perry's," he said, all innocent.

"No, you aren't. Mama told me you had to stay home."

"Down to Perry's is practically stayin' home."

"You just want to tell him about Jesse."

He didn't say anything and I knew I was right. He went out the front door and stood on the porch.

"Don't you leave the yard," I said.

Just like I thought, a storm hit by early evening. Before I could worry about Mama getting soaked on her walk home, I heard a car approaching. The same car from last night. Dr. Montgomery had driven Mama home. Now she jumped out of the car and ran for the porch, calling her thanks over her shoulder.

She came in shaking her hat and wiping her wet face. "Hi, Mama," I said and began to set the table. Prez came out from the back room. "Hi, Mama," he said sheepishly.

"Boy, don't you know I could hardly work today, thinkin' about last night?" She sat down heavily at the table and I brought her her dinner. Prez went to the window and looked toward the shed. Then he looked pointedly at me. Mama felt our tension.

"What's with you two?"

"Nothing," I said, and shot Prez a warning look.

"Get your rest tonight, Francie. We got Miss Rivers' house in the morning."

Mentally, I sighed. I'd left Jesse alone all day, thinking he was exhausted from the night before. But I'd sure planned to sneak him some dinner before Mama got back from the Montgomerys'. Because of the storm, she'd gotten back sooner than expected. Now she was going to make sure I got into bed early.

"Prez," I said, pulling him aside as soon as I could, "when Mama and I leave in the morning, you take Jesse something to eat."

He stared at me stupidly. "Don't forget," I said.

"Get your clothes on, Francie. And hurry."

I sulked all the way there. When we had stepped out into the yard, I snuck a quick peek at the shed. Oddly, I felt no sense of Jesse. It was almost as if he wasn't there.

"Put that lip back in, missy. I ain't gonna have you walk around all morning with a long face, spoilin' everybody's happiness."

Miss Rivers taught history at the white high school. She had a regular maid, Burnette, who was all the time putting on airs. She pointedly called herself a housekeeper. And she thought she was a step up from us because she was lighter and Miss Rivers had taken her along to Paris a few summers back.

She'd come back practically thinking she was French. All the time slipping in little tidbits about "gay *Paree*" and how the men thought of her as exotic. "Exoteek," as she said it. "They didn't think I was no African, neither," she'd said to me and Mama on one of our workdays there at Miss Rivers'.

Burnette opened the back door and gave us the full inspection. We wouldn't have to serve at this function; we'd just be doing the cleaning and cooking. Which was fine with me because then I could eat a little bit as I prepared things. It was easier than serving. More relaxing. And Bea Mosely was there already and she always kept me and Mama in stitches.

We stepped through the door. Burnette shook her head. "Didn't you bring something to put on your hair?" Mama pulled off her hat and smoothed her hair.

"I'll just have to find you something. You can't prepare food with your hair uncovered. It's not sanitary." She sashayed out of the kitchen. Miss Bea looked back at me and Mama and we all burst into laughter. "I guess she told you," Miss Bea said.

"I guess she did," Mama agreed, not caring a whit.

"Well, I'm glad you're here, because she like to drive me out of my mind."

"So now she can drive us all out of our minds."

Burnette came back with two kerchiefs. Mama and I tied them on and then followed her to the dining room to get the rug up and outside. It was heavy and hard to get over the railing evenly. Once I had it up there, Mama handed me the broom and told me to sweep the porch.

As I neared the end of the back side of the porch, I heard Sheriff Barnes's voice coming from around the corner.

"I'ma get going, Miss Rivers."

"Well, tell Mrs. Barnes we're sure going to miss her today and we're sorry she's down with that cold."

"Will do. Just as soon as I get back from out Three Notch way."

I stopped sweeping the porch.

"What do you have to do out there?" Miss Rivers asked.

"I'm not satisfied with our search yet. I want to check some sheds and chicken coops and under a few corncribs . . . I got me a hunch."

"Well, I suppose you've got to go with a hunch. They usually pay off."

I heard the sheriff go down the steps, and peeked around the corner just as he was getting in his car. I watched him ease out of Miss Rivers' driveway, then I looked back at Mama—the edge of her scarf already a dark ring of sweat—and knew what I was going to do. I quickly swept around the corner of the porch and out of sight. Mama had glanced over at me once, but her mind seemed to be on something else. I leaned the broom against the porch railing, and went down the steps and across the front lawn toward the road. Then I ran.

I'd been walking for some time and still had a long way to go when a horn made me jump. I was afraid to turn around until I heard a friendly voice. "Where you going so fast, Francie?" It was Mr. Grandy. I hurried to the cab of the truck, gripping the windowsill.

"Something's come up and I need a ride back home, Mr. Grandy."

"Well, hop in."

"Thank you, sir."

Mr. Grandy began to speak the moment I settled in the seat. "You over your fright by now? Shame how those boys put you through all that—"

"Yes, Mr. Grandy," I said, cutting him off. "But that's done now."

We rode along in silence for a bit. Then I thought of something. "Mr. Grandy—that hobo camp—is it still down there by the viaduct?"

"I wouldn't know. I ain't been down that way."

I thought about Alberta and her cap pulled down to her eyebrows. Mr. Grandy was wearing the same kind of cap. I felt a small desire to dress up in men's clothes and be gone myself. I wouldn't need to take much, neither. Just some of my books. I was so tired of working and having no friends to be with and nothing ahead of me each day but drudgery . . . But it wasn't myself I was thinking of when I asked about the hoboes. That Alberta girl—she seemed to know all about hopping freights. She could help Jesse get to California.

Mr. Grandy pulled in front of my house and I jumped out. "Thank you, Mr. Grandy. I appreciate it." I waited until he drove away before I headed for the shed.

The door was ajar. That in itself signaled that something was amiss. I eased the door open and peered in. Mama's quilt, the pillow, the book, the jars of food—all of it was gone. There was no sign of hurry or struggle.

I looked around in the shed and the house for something that would give me a clue as to where Jesse'd gone. There was nothing, no footprints on the shed's dirt floor, none of the things I'd given him left behind. He'd just up and left. Went back to the woods, I guessed. I felt a mixture of relief and disappointment. What was I supposed to do now?

I'd have to make that long trek back to Miss Rivers' and face Mama's wrath. I had a good mind to go to my hill with a book. If I was going to get in trouble, I might as well really deserve it.

But I didn't. I turned up the road toward Ambrose Park. I'd barely gotten past Miss Mabel's when I heard her screen door slam and my name called.

"You missed all the excitement," she yelled.

I stopped in my tracks and went to stand in front of her porch steps.

"Pardon me, Miss Mabel?"

"Sheriff Barnes was out here." She smacked her lips a bit, taking her time. "Searching for that boy." She took a bite of biscuit. I waited while she gummed it. "Went over to your place and looked in your shed."

"They go in?" I asked, remembering the smooth floor.

"I know he looked in. Looked under the corncrib, too. Then he came on down here. Course he know better than to think I'd be hidin' anybody. I got some sense."

I wondered briefly if she knew that Jesse Pruitt had slept in our shed.

"Then he went on down to the Grandys'," Miss Mabel was saying.

I looked in that direction in search of the sheriff's car. It wasn't there.

"Oh, he ain't down there now. He was heading down to the Tallys' last I saw. Probably go on down to the Darnells' next. Where you off to?" she asked quickly before I could get away.

"Mama's cooking over at Miss Rivers' in Ambrose Park. I gotta go," I said. "She's waiting on me." That wasn't a lie. She was probably waiting on me, all right—with her belt.

I got back just as Mama was coming out to empty a bucket of sudsy water in the bushes. Mama glanced in my direction, then did a double take.

"Francie Weaver!" She caught me by the shoulder and dug her nails into my flesh through my shirtsleeve.

"Just where have you *been*! You had me worried sick—just leavin' the broom leanin' against the rail without even a by-your-leave." She pushed me along. "I ain't got time to beat your butt now, but know this—your behind is mine!"

Which meant I had to spend the rest of the afternoon working in the awful knowledge that I had a whipping ahead of me. No matter how fast and efficiently I did my job for the rest of the day, I was going to get what I was owed, so everything seemed pretty useless. Burnette gave me a whole tray of glasses back, saying I'd left lint in them and they weren't fit to return to the china cabinet.

I used my hip to open the door to the kitchen and eased into the room with the heavy tray. Bea Mosely, standing at the sink, looked over her shoulder and said, "What you bring those back for?"

"Burnette said I left lint on them."

Bea Mosely rolled her eyes at that. "Leave 'em. I'll take care of it. Your mama's waitin' on the porch for you anyhow."

I set the tray on the table and slowly slipped off my apron and kerchief.

"Bye, Miss Bea," I said before going out the door.

Mama was sitting on the back steps, staring off toward Miss Rivers' rose garden. "I always wanted me a rose garden," she said as she got up heavily. She seemed to have lost all her anger.

We started up Parker Street, then turned down Mrs. Montgomery's street. Clarissa was playing cards with some girls on her porch. One lifted her clinking glass of iced tea to her lips and took a long sip. The heat and stagnant air felt burdensome. Mama and I had a long, long walk ahead of us home to Three Notch. I would have waved to Clarissa—she'd been so nice to me, then Prez and Perry, too—but her back was to me.

Mama's voice dispelled the silence between us, surprising me. "I believe you must've had some good reason to run off that way. I'ma listen to what you have to say before I decide whether or not to give you your whippin'." She looked over at me, waiting.

"I had to go back home, Mama."

"I know you gonna tell me why . . ."

"I heard Sheriff Barnes telling Miss Rivers he was going out our way to search barns and corncribs and such."

"What's goin' on, Francie . . ."

"I hid Jesse in the shed."

Mama stopped in her tracks.

"I had to, Mama. He was so pitiful when he came out of the woods, and I was so glad to see that he wasn't hurt bad or dead."

Mama began walking again. "Where's he now?"

"I don't know, Mama. I think he left before the sheriff ever got there. I got a ride home with Mr. Grandy and there wasn't not one sign of Jesse in that shed. I think he's gone."

We walked on in silence.

"What if Daddy don't ever send for us, Mama?" I knew

I was breaking an unspoken rule, saying that, but I had to ask.

Mama was silent.

"He didn't come when he said he was," I persisted. "How we know he's gonna send for us just cause he said he would? We don't even have a date. People probably think we ain't going nowhere."

"Those are the jealous folks. They're like crawdads in a barrel. They don't want no one gettin' out if they can't."

"But, Mama—"

"You got to be patient," Mama said. "God willing, we're moving . . ."

"Mama, I think only you believe that."

"Just have faith."

I didn't get the promised whipping. When we reached home, she told me to go on in and start supper, she was just going to sit on the porch swing and rest a bit.

Prez hadn't gotten home yet from down to Auntie's. He was supposed to be helping Perry fix the chicken coop, but I knew they'd probably done just as much play as work, and they'd be in a rush to get something finished before the sun set.

I got the dinner going and came out to sit by Mama. She was staring at the mailbox. "I'm so sick of workin' on Sundays. Wish I had me one Sunday where I could go to church and pray to God. The white ladies make sure they go, before they have their teas and luncheons and book clubs . . ."

I studied Mama's wistful face. I almost never saw her looking like this. And talking about what she wished for. Mama just worked—all the time. Her harsh words probably came out of her weariness, mostly. Mama loved us, I knew. "Tonight, before we go to bed—we'll say a special prayer to God for Jesse."

"Mama."

"Yes, baby."

"God will hear us, no matter where we pray."

"That sure is true."

It was then that we noticed the flag up on the mailbox. How could we miss it? We both looked at it for a bit. "We got mail," Mama said. "Go see what we got."

Word from Daddy

I already knew it was from Daddy. I didn't feel good about it, for some reason. I carried it back to Mama and held it out. She must have felt it, too, because she was slow to take it out of my hand. I followed her to the house. We settled at the table. "Go on—read it," she said, sighing.

I opened it and a ten-dollar bill fell out. My throat grew tight over the first few sentences.

Dear Family:

I pray this letter finds you all in good health and doing well. I'm sorry I couldn't get word to you that I wasn't able to come like I planned. I sure hope this letter gets to you directly and you didn't go to too much trouble. I know it must have been a disappointment. Family, this letter brings bad news. We're going to have to put off your move up here for a little while longer. I think I'll have the money to get you up here by spring . . .

I stopped reading then. Spring was past. The spring he was talking about was next *year*! *Next year!*

I threw the letter down on the table. Tears collected in my eyes, then rolled down my cheeks. It wasn't fair . . .

"Finish reading, Francie," Mama said.

I finished all the pointless stuff about how hot and humid Chicago was, how hard Daddy's last run was. How tired he was. And I thought, maybe he did have another family. Mama held out her hand. I put the letter in it and watched her fold it in half. She got up and put it on the pantry shelf in the little box with all the others.

It had been so long since we'd seen him. I closed my eyes, trying to picture his face. I couldn't see it.

Prez cried when he heard the news later. His wails did the job for me and Mama both, I was certain. It wasn't until I was in bed that I cried so hard I thought I'd make myself sick. I could hear Mama out on the porch. The slow creaking of the swing sounded sad and hopeless.

Mama let me sleep. When I woke, my face felt swollen from a night of determined crying. I sat up and tried to remember when and how I'd finally fallen asleep. I had no memory of Mama coming to bed. I had no memory of Mama getting up to fix breakfast. Yet the table was laid out with all our favorites when I dragged myself into the kitchen.

Mama sat at the table. "Are you hungry?"

I shrugged. I was hungry, having refused dinner the night before—but I didn't want to admit it. Prez came in then, his eyes red and watery.

"We ain't never movin' to be with Daddy," he said.

Mama just got up and dished grits onto our plates and scrambled eggs and biscuits with butter and peach preserves. I began to eat hungrily. I wasn't going to care. What was the point? I was too angry to worry about Jesse, who was probably long gone anyway, who knew where. Jesse hadn't cared enough to say thank you or even goodbye—so why should I care?

"Francie, what's taking you so long?" Mama stood at the bottom of Miss Beach's back stairs, calling up to me. I ignored her first call and hovered over Miss Lafayette's dresser some more. She'd gone into town, so I didn't even have her to talk to.

She had a new photograph up there and I was studying it. Her beau, I decided. Her fiancé. He was going to marry her and take her away from Noble. Judging from his clothes, I decided he was a man of means and intelligence and education. Just the kind of man I hoped to meet and marry one day, God willing. He wouldn't be no railroad man.

" 'Bout time," Miss Beach said to me nastily, her face

full of suspicion as she watched me drop the load of clothes and sheets onto the floor with the other loads. "What were you doing up there, anyway?"

"Nothing. Just getting the linens."

"Took you long enough. You better not have been up there messing in people's things."

Mama looked over. "Francie knows better not to mess with nothing that don't belong to her," she said, sending a tiny jolt of guilt through me.

Treasure trotted by and rubbed his back on Miss Beach's leg, signaling to be picked up. She brought his tiny face close to hers and began cooing at him almost nose to nose until her teakettle went off. Then she let him slip back to the floor. He leaped right into the middle of Mama's pile of whites, nestled down, and settled his head on his paws. He blinked up at me. Mama frowned at him.

"Scoot," she said and motioned with her hand.

He squinted at me again and yawned. "Go on, cat," Mama said and waved at him again. Miss Beach stood at the stove, slowly dunking her tea bag in her cup.

"Come on, now . . ." Mama said and pulled a little at the corner of the top sheet. It only budged him momentarily from his roosting post. He wiggled back to it stubbornly. I hated him more than ever. Miss Beach continued stirring her tea, with her back to us. Around and around went her spoon.

Real fast, I yanked the corner of the sheet, sending the

cat sailing across the kitchen, then landing with a wonderful thud. Miss Beach whirled her fat self around then, her eyes popping out at Treasure heaped in the corner of the kitchen. He unfurled, stood up, and gave himself a little shake.

"What did you do to my cat?" she gasped.

"Just moved him off the sheet," I said, pleased with myself.

"You did more than that." She watched him wobble to the table and scamper underneath it. "I see why he doesn't like you. You're mean and evil to him."

"He scratches me for no good reason."

"I don't believe that for a second. If you'll steal, you'll lie."

"When did I steal?"

"One half can of smoked salmon."

"I never stole no salmon."

"Last week I left a half can on the sideboard for my lunch. I left the room and when I came back it was finished off."

"It was probably that crazy cat of yours." I shook with anger. I looked over at Mama, but she was just sorting the clothes, keeping her eyes on her task.

"You think cause you're moving North that you can do whatever you please . . . Well, let me tell you, Miss Ann."

"That ain't true," I said back. "Cause we ain't even going." I said it quickly before thinking, then immediately wished I could pull those words out of the air and put them back in my mouth.

Miss Beach latched onto that, lifted an eyebrow—looked from me to Mama and back to me, her lips a quivering little smile. "Oh?"

Mama threw me a scathing look.

"What's this? No move to Chicago? I knew it! Course I didn't want to say anything, with you all being so sure and all." She sat down to get comfortable. Mama just continued to sort. "Well, what happened, Lil? What happened to the big move?"

Without looking up, Mama said, "It's been delayed."

"Delayed." Miss Beach brought her cup to her lips and blew. "I see. Well, I'm sure it's just as well. Things can be hard up there—for country folk. It ain't the paradise people say it is and . . ." She stopped then. Mama had gathered the first load and was heading out the door.

"Why'd you tell that woman we weren't going?" Mama growled at me as we were wringing the sheets.

"It just came out."

"Yea? Well, now it's going to be *out* all over town."

We got the laundry hung on the lines and settled on the porch steps to eat our lunch. Miss Beach opened the door behind us. "Since you aren't movin' anywhere, I'm gonna need you in a few weeks to get at my attic. It'll be a major job. Maybe take a week or two." When Mama didn't say anything, Miss Beach said, "You'll be able to do it, won't you?"

"I can't be sure, Miss Beach." I looked over at Mama, surprised. Mama didn't refuse work unless she was sick or someone in the family needed her. "I can tell you next week—about September."

About September. What did Mama mean by that.

I could tell Miss Beach was puzzled, too. She just sputtered. "Well, I must know by next week at the latest—I have to make my plans, you know."

"God willing, you'll know by next week."

Crawdads

A bleak week followed. I could hardly go through the motions: Tuesday, helping serve at Mrs. Montgomery's book club; Wednesday, serving at a tea at some friend of Mrs. Grace's; Thursday, cooking and doing laundry at Auntie's. She continued to feel better, but still needed help. Every once in a while, I'd look up from stirring the diapers over the open fire outside and check the woods and think: Where are you, Jesse—where are you? Not knowing was nearly unbearable. The thought of staying in Noble for almost another year was nearly as unbearable. God, please help me get through all of this, I prayed.

Mama must have seen the sad look on my face. Friday, she gave me a day off. I had to go to my hill. It had been days and days since I'd been there.

. . .

The hoboes were cooking one of their stews. Its strong aroma drifted up the hillside where I sat with my Scooter Pie in my lap still in its cellophane wrapper. I didn't want to eat it yet. Sometimes the moment just didn't seem right and I liked to wait.

I was watching Alberta, anyway, wondering if she'd ever had a chance to get away. She was squatting by the river, washing a shirt with a slow, tired rhythm. She wrung it, stood up, and with her dripping garment in one hand and her other hand shading her eyes, she looked right up at me and smiled brightly. There was a small shadow in her mouth like she'd lost a tooth. She began the climb up to me.

"Hey," she said when she reached me. It was a front tooth, but I wasn't going to ask her about it and embarrass her. "You lookin' for your train?"

"Yea . . . " I squinted up at her in her man's cap. "They don't know you're a girl yet?"

"I guess they do—but they don't pay no attention to me." She sunk down beside me.

I sat up straight and stared at her. "Weren't you going to California?"

"I didn't make it. I just come back from New Orleans."

"Why'd you come *back*?"

"Just wanted to."

I wondered what was the real reason.

"I was workin', too, in a big house there. I earned me some money."

"Alberta, don't you have family?" I had to ask her this, though I feared it would make her feel funny.

"I have family." Her eyes hardened. "I just didn't get along with my stepdaddy. He was mean—especially when he drank."

As casually as possible, I asked, "Have you seen a colored boy around here looking to get down to New Orleans?"

"The one they're after?" she answered, surprising me. She looked at me sharply. "Why?"

"I know him. And—I want to know if he's okay."

She waited so long I didn't think I was going to get an answer. "I ain't seen him," she finally said.

We sat quietly for a while. Someone down there had picked up a harmonica and music reached up to us. Alberta tapped her booted foot.

"I might go back down to New Orleans. It's nice."

"Ain't you ever going to settle down?"

"Yea. When I get good and ready." She stood up and brushed off the back of her trousers. "I gotta go," she said, then started back down the hill.

I watched her, thinking how easily she left people. No goodbye. Just like Jesse. He never did say goodbye, he always just left.

"Here, take this out to the back porch and sweep it good," Burnette said to me. It was Saturday. We were back at Miss Rivers' for heavy cleaning, and Burnette was being particularly bossy. I felt her watching me as I started for the door. "Wait a minute."

I looked back at her, waiting.

"I hear you ain't going up to Chicago after all—least not anytime soon . . ." A smile played on her lips. I went out the door without speaking and started my sweeping. Miss Rivers was visiting with her sister. They sat at a little table under her big live oak, having tea and cake. What was it like to wake up every morning and have only pleasantness to fill your day? To have not a speck of work to think of? To have money enough to hire people to take care of all that you didn't want no part of? I might as well have wondered what it was like living on Mars.

After sweeping, I went in, so Burnette could tell me what my next task would be. Mama had sent me to Miss Rivers' in her stead, saying she had things to do. Strange behavior for Mama. What could she have to do? Auntie was feeling better, Baby Janie was fine. I thought about her being born between the two lights, and almost slipped into ignorance and superstition before I could catch myself.

"Come on in here, Miss Ann," Burnette said, motioning to me from her comfortable seat at the table. She was sipping iced tea. She tinkled the ice cubes in her tall glass while she thought. "You need to get started on the parlor windows." She nodded at the supplies lined up on the counter. "You need to take your time and don't leave streaks."

"Yes, ma'am."

"Why'd your mama send you, anyway? Miss Rivers wanted your mama, not you."

"She said me coming was okay."

"But what's your mama got to do that so important that she couldn't come herself?"

"I don't know."

"Or you don't want to say." She took a sip of tea and cocked her head to the side. "Your mama better be careful to keep people like Miss Rivers happy. Looks like she's gonna be dependin' on her for *employment* for a little while longer."

"Yes, ma'am," I said, gathering the bucket and vinegar and newspapers. The sooner I got those windows done and got out of there, the better.

I took my time going home. I felt no rush. Why should I? What was there? I looked through the heat shimmering just above the road ahead of me. My throat closed and tears came to my eyes. Nothing ever went right for long. Just like Jesse. I remembered the sad sight of his back moving away from me as he made his way toward our shed. He'd stopped then to readjust his load and for a moment I'd considered calling out just to prolong the sight of him. You never knew if you'd never lay eyes on a person again.

When I last saw Daddy—last summer—and he kissed

me goodbye and said "See you soon," I believed I'd see him soon. Not that a whole year would go by. He might as well have stayed at the pulp mill. He might as well have never promised to go up there to Chicago and pave the way for our new life.

I heard my name called then. I was coming up to Miss Mabel's. She sat back in the shadow of her porch, almost hidden. I wanted to keep going, but home training made me turn into her yard. I put my hands behind my back.

"Hey, Miss Mabel. How are you this evening?"

"Mmmm," she started, thinking. And I knew she was going to list her ailments. "I've done better, but I don't like to complain." Her chair scraped. "Come on up here and visit awhile."

"I gotta get home and start supper."

There was a moment of dead silence in which I sensed her caginess.

"I hear you all ain't going up there to Chicago. I hope you don't mind me telling you—I never did think you were going anywhere. Men always telling their family they gonna go on ahead to get things situated, and they don't ever do nothin' but keep 'em hangin' around the mailbox looking for train tickets that ain't never gonna come." She licked her lips and nodded. "I seen it happen over and over."

All the time she was talking, I felt my heart hardening into stone and an awful pain starting in my head. Before I could stop myself, harsh words poured out of my mouth.

"You just the meanest ol' woman I ever knew—saying those awful things to me. I believe you love other folks' misery. I believe it makes you happy. What kind of God-fearing woman are you to be so happy about our disappointment . . ."

"Why, you hateful, hateful child," she called out to me as I walked toward our house. The words were hitting my back, but I didn't really feel anything. My legs felt heavy as lead. I didn't even know I was crying until the tears were tickling my chin. Not even when Daddy didn't show did I feel this bitterly disappointed.

I couldn't go in the house when I reached it. It was empty and sad. Prez had yet to come home from the Early farm and Mama had said she'd be gone all day. Maybe she was over at Auntie's by now. I sat on the top porch step and stared at our mailbox with its flag down. No mail. No nothing.

In the last light, I saw Mama coming up the road. She had on her town hat—which she wouldn't have worn to Auntie's—and a big box under her arm.

"Evenin', Francie," she said, climbing the steps and going past me into the house.

I barely got out an "Evenin', Mama." Something was up.

I followed close on her heels. She took off her hat and hung it on its hook, then looked around. "You ain't started supper."

"I was just getting to it."

"Prez ain't back yet?"

"He's been hanging out at Auntie's after he gets done at the Earlys'."

Mama sighed. She went over to our bed and slipped the big box under it. Before I could ask her what was in it, she said, "How was it at Miss Rivers'?"

"Burnette was happy to lord it over me. I think she even gave me some of her chores, since you weren't there to know what was her work and what was yours. I did the parlor windows, swept and washed the whole veranda. Waxed the parlor floor and the entire staircase and—"

"What's done is done," Mama said. "You weren't there to wax no floors, but I'll straighten that out with Miss Rivers before we move."

Move. What was Mama talking about? *Move.* She smoothed her skirt and went over to the basin to wash her face and hands.

"First thing Monday," she said, patting her face dry, "you're going to go down to Green's—you and Prez—and you're going to bring back as many boxes as you can carry. We got some packin' to do. We giving everything we're not taking to Chicago to Auntie."

Mama's Got Plans

I had not heard her right. I stared at her, waiting for further explanation. How could we just up and move before Daddy had arranged for us to come?

"But, Mama . . ."

"Don't ask me no questions—I'm not gonna be answering any." She got busy then, starting our supper. I kept quiet, happy Mama had the energy to get supper and relieve me.

"What you think she's gonna do, Francie?" Prez asked me. We were sitting on the porch, watching Juniper lap furiously at his bowl of water. He'd just gulped down a moth and it must have been hot like pepper. I laughed, then Prez joined in. Juniper looked so pitiful.

"She's not saying. And when Mama says she's not saying . . . she's *not* saying."

"How can we move up there when Daddy ain't sent for us?"

"She's got *something* in mind. I know it."

We were coming back with our boxes. I got Vell to give us all that we could carry. We could hardly see for what was stacked in our arms.

"Where you going with them boxes?" It was Miss Mabel. Was there a nosier woman on earth?

"We movin'!" Prez shouted out before I could jab him in the side.

"Movin'!" Miss Mabel got up off her chair then and came to the edge of the porch. She held on to her post and watched us, her mouth hanging open.

"Shut up," I hissed at Prez.

"We movin' to Chicago, *anyhow*!" Prez shouted.

"That's it. I'm telling on you. I'm telling Mama you telling the whole world our business."

He didn't care. He was revved up. I might as well have said nothing.

We stacked the boxes on our porch, then I looked down toward Auntie's house. "Stay out here," I ordered Prez. "And watch for Mama." I wanted to see what was in that box under the bed.

I pulled it out and stared down at it for a few seconds. I lifted off the top and saw something soft and blue peeking out from the tissue paper it was wrapped in. I peeled back one corner of the paper. Rhinestone buttons glittered in a row down a bodice front. The skirt was folded underneath. It was a new dress for Mama. I'd never known her to buy one.

Mama came home after dark. I was surprised to see her in her work dress. She hadn't said anything about working.

Still wearing her hat, she walked over to the table and placed a shiny fifty-cent piece in the middle of it. "That's yours, Francie."

"For what?"

"That extra work you did at Miss Rivers'. I collected what was owed."

I slipped it in my pocket. I wasn't going to buy any Scooter Pies with it, either. I was saving it for Chicago. No telling what I'd want to buy up there.

"Now come here, you two. I got something to show you."

She led us over to the bed and reached down and pulled out her box. She set it on the bed, carefully lifted off the lid, and pushed back the paper. "It's the dress I intend to wear up to Chicago. The one your daddy's gonna see me in first off." She held it up to her chin and smiled happily. I'd never seen her smile like that before. Prez and I looked at each other.

"It's real pretty, Mama," Prez said first.

"It's real pretty," I agreed.

She went over to the wardrobe and opened the curtain. She fished around on the bottom of it and pulled out two more boxes. One she handed to Prez—then one to me. I almost stopped breathing. Prez dropped to his knees and ripped off the top. "New pants and shirt!" he cried. "Can I try 'em on?"

"Not till you have a bath."

I sat down on the edge of the bed to open my box. My heart pounded, my eyes welled up. I felt such happiness and fear all mixed up. We *were* going . . . but how? I pulled a yellow eyelet dress out. It was so beautiful. My favorite color.

"You like it?" Mama asked.

I could only nod.

"Good. We're leaving on Saturday."

"How, Mama?"

"By train."

"Daddy sent the tickets?"

"No. I went and bought them myself—with money I been settin' aside." She pulled herself up straighter. "Now don't ask me any more. Just do as I tell you."

Everything was a whirl thereafter. Prez was down to Perry's night and day; they suddenly were joined at the hip, realizing they would soon be parted. And Mama was down there, too, helping Auntie get ready for her move up to Benson.

Mama had sent a telegram to Daddy to tell him we were coming and he just better get ready for us. And he better meet our train. Pulling in Sunday morning.

Lots of stuff we were giving to Auntie, who was going to have a larger household up in Benson. The furniture was staying because it wasn't ours. It all belonged to the white family we rented from. But that didn't matter none. When we got to Chicago and finally moved into our own house, we'd be buying all new.

Moving Day

We'd been in a rush all morning, scared we were going to miss the local for sure—and our connection in Birmingham. I'd never seen Mama in such a state. She paced. She stammered out instructions. "Prez, you need to get Juniper over to Auntie's before Uncle June gets here. Francie, don't take them rags out of your hair until the last minute. Prez, don't walk so hard—you gonna make Daddy's cake fall."

She'd fried a chicken for the trip, then worried that the grease smell had gotten into her hair. She'd yelled at me for having my nose stuck in my book of poetry by Langston Hughes, even though there wasn't really anything that she had for me to do. We'd done it all. She'd made up her face twice, but the sweat was still pouring off in little streams down her powdered cheeks. Finally, she decided to just scrub her face, dab on a little lipstick, and let it be.

In the excitement of the past few days, Mama had been eating like a bird and had lost weight from her nerves. Now, at last, she sunk down at the kitchen table and sipped coffee, her eyes glassy with tears.

I went over to her and hugged her. "It's gonna be okay, Mama." The few suitcases and parcels we were taking were out on the porch, waiting on Uncle June. Mr. Griffin, our landlord, had already come by to look at the house and determine that we weren't leaving it any worse for wear and we weren't hauling off any of the few sticks of furniture that had come with the house. He had stomped off grim and in a bad mood. He hated to lose a tenant who'd always had that rent money in his hand on the first of every month, rain or shine.

Mama got up to pace some more. "Uncle June's gonna make us late for our train for sure if he don't get here soon," she said, staring out the window, then turning her worried face back to me. I felt calm, though I could hardly imagine not spending any more of my life within these walls. I felt guilty that I wasn't sadder than I was.

Prez, in his excitement about Chicago, was only sad about leaving Perry and Juniper. He'd finally gone to take poor Juniper down to Auntie's, and then he'd be coming back with Uncle June.

I got up and moved to our bed to sit on it for the last

time. My throat got tight and my eyes welled. While I sat on the bare mattress, I dropped my face in my hands and cried.

We were leaving *everything*. And what were we going to do? What if we couldn't get used to such a big place? What if Chicago coloreds laughed at us? We wouldn't talk like them or dress like them.

And Daddy had already told me I'd be going to school with white children. Sitting right next to them in the classroom—learning what they were learning. I couldn't imagine such a thing.

I ran my hand over the mattress. My last time sitting on this bed . . . my last time.

A loud horn sounded. "Uncle June's here!" Mama called out from the porch, where she'd gone to check on our belongings. "Hurry, Francie—we gotta get going. Help me get our things out to the car."

Mama was bending over the bulging bags and cases on the porch and rearranging stuff. The cake and fried chicken and potato salad and pickled peaches and jars of lemonade were boxed and tied with string. I'd left out the *War and Peace* Clarissa gave me. I planned to start it on the train. I should have said goodbye to her. And to Serena and Miss Lafayette, too. I was as bad as Jesse and Alberta—just moving on like I was. Just pointing all my attention on what was ahead and almost forgetting about who and what I was leaving behind. Even the jars still in the woods. We'd be long gone by the time anyone found them.

I had on my new yellow dress. I'd pulled the rags out of my hair, and greasy curls that I wasn't to comb out until just before we reached the station covered my head. Prez and Perry leaned their heads out of the car. Auntie, with Janie on her lap, scooted close to Uncle June to make room for Mama. Prez jumped out and shouted, "Come on and get in, slowpoke."

Uncle June, in clean overalls and a big-brimmed hat, got out and opened the trunk for our belongings. "Hey, Miss Priss." He smiled down at me. "You ready to leave Noble?"

"I think so," I said, my voice sounding uncertain to my own ears.

"We sure gonna miss you," he said.

I smiled and got into the car, pushing Prez on the shoulder so he would give me more room. The car started up with a noise that was like a loud horse's snort. We moved out over the bumpy road. I looked out the window at the fields beginning to race by. The woods whizzed goodbye.

"We going on a train!" Prez said, punching Perry in the shoulder softly. The grownups in the front seat laughed. I looked out the back window then to say goodbye to the house on Three Notch Road, secretly.

Mr. Grandy was coming up behind us. He honked.

"Uncle June, Mr. Grandy wants us," I said. "Uncle June, pull over."

Uncle June stopped the car and all of us looked back

and watched Mr. Grandy climb out of his truck and walk over to us. "I thought that was you, June." I noticed a small envelope in his hand. "How you doin' up there in Benson?"

"Doin' pretty good. Finally movin' my family up there."

"I heard. We all gonna miss Lil and Lydia, and the children, too."

My eyes latched onto the envelope he was using to gesture with. "How you doin'?" he asked Mama and Auntie.

"Fine," Mama said, speaking up first. "Just trying to get to our train before it go off and leave us."

"Oh, sure," Mr. Grandy said, bringing the letter up near his eyes. "I saw this being put in your mailbox right after you pulled away. Francie almost missed it." He handed it to me while everyone turned their puzzled faces to me. I checked the postmark, just as puzzled. California. My breath quickened. All waited. Mama and Auntie and Uncle June had practically turned all the way around in their seats.

"It's from California," I said.

"California," they said together.

Mama recovered first. "Open it, Francie. See who it's from."

I knew who it was from. Even before I tore off the end of the envelope, blew in it, and let the contents fall in my lap. Prez tried to grab the postcard that had fallen out, but I was quicker.

It was just a picture postcard. Of an orange grove. For the second time that day, my eyes filled with tears, and I looked out the window to hide my face, then realized Mr. Grandy was out that window, looking right at me.

"Who's it from?" Mama said impatiently.

I brought the envelope up to my face as if I didn't know and had to read the return address. Of course there wasn't one. My name was written in a child's script, full of struggle, it looked like. Then: Three Notch Road. Then: Noble, Alabama. Jesse hadn't been in school long enough to learn to write. Someone must have helped him.

"You gonna tell us who that postcard's from, Francie?" Uncle June asked.

"It's from Jesse Pruitt," I said.

Mama opened her mouth, but nothing came out. Auntie looked at Uncle June, and Prez and Perry said "Wow!" at the same time.

"He got himself out to California," I said.

"Well, why you crying?" Mama asked.

"I didn't think he ever would . . ."

Mama smiled at me. Mr. Grandy backed away from the car and let us get going. He waved at us and we waved back. I slipped the postcard in my *War and Peace*, deciding I was going to use it for my new bookmark. That way, I'd be looking at that picture of oranges growing on trees for a long, long time and thinking about Jesse *making it* and deciding—I could, too.